MW00531854

THE KILLER KNIGHT AND THE MURDEROUS CHAIRLEG

POINT MUSE COZY PARANORMAL MYSTERY: BOOK ONE

KELLY ETHAN

Copyright © 2021 by Kelly Ethan

All rights reserved.

No part of this book may be reproduced in any form or by any electronic or mechanical means, including information storage and retrieval systems, without written permission from the author, except for the use of brief quotations in a book review.

Publisher's Note: This is a work of fiction. Names, characters, places, and incidents are a product of the author's imagination. Locales and public names are sometimes used for atmospheric purposes. Any resemblance to actual people, living or dead, or to businesses, companies, events, institutions, or locales is completely coincidental.

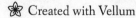 Created with Vellum

*Love and hugs to Alexis Fleming. Sometimes it takes
a village to produce a book baby.*

*Special shout out to Barbara, Becky Neilsen and
Theresa, my amazing proofreaders. You made my
book baby glow. Big hugs.*

*And to my ARC Team who have eagle eyes for typos
as well. You all rock!*

THE KILLER KNIGHT AND THE MURDEROUS CHAIRLEG

POINT MUSE COZY PARANORMAL MYSTERY: BOOK ONE

There's a murder in the library, a killer knight stalking victims and a nosy librarian turned sleuth.

Let the mayhem begin...

Xandie Meyers thought all her troubles were over when she moved to Point Muse, Maine. Instead, she inherited her Great-Aunt's supernatural library and a snarky, talking cat. Not to mention a family of chaos-causing witches, furry law enforcement and a card-carrying demon from hell...and a dead body.

Xandie Myers is suspect number one, and she has no clue who's targeting her. Sherlock librarian needs to swing into action and sniff the real killer out before she becomes the next victim—or ends up in jail for murders she didn't commit.

Can Xandie survive long enough to navigate her freaky new world? Or will things that go bump in the night have her for a midnight snack?

If you like snarky dialogue, murder, and mayhem then you'll love the next instalment in Kelly Ethan's Point Muse Mysteries, a new cozy paranormal mystery series.

Unlock the mayhem of The Killer Knight and the Murderous Chairleg!

ONE

"Let me guess. The feline knocked my great-aunt Sera off?" Alexandra 'Xandie' Meyers glared at the evil, murderous feline locked away in his cat cage jail. The black monster hissed and stuck a paw out with claws extended, waving in her direction.

"Of course not. Theo's a placid animal. But he's taken a mild dislike to you." The lawyer mopped his shiny brow and offered a weak smile.

"Mild?" Xandie winced as she tracked the red, angry scratch trailing from her wrist to halfway up her arm. "I don't remember him being this nasty when I visited Aunt Sera last."

"I'm sure Theo's disturbed by the events of the last week. Your great-aunt's death shocked the town.

Point Muse loved Sera." The lawyer rifled through his bag until he found an old-fashioned set of heavy keys. "Here you go. Keys to the house. Any questions please call my office." He shoved the keys at Xandie and hustled off the front porch.

Anyone might think he was desperate to leave. "Ah, thanks, Mr. Essam."

"It's Neville," he yelled over his shoulder as he clambered into his car and roared out of the driveway, spraying dust along the way.

"Who could forget Mr. Neville 'Run Away' Essam? You'd think I had the plague." Xandie contemplated her inheritance. The house was lovely, red brick and wood, gables galore and a long wide porch on the front, the whole thing set on two lovely green acres. What wasn't nice was the spitting, murder-minded cat she'd inherited from Sera. Xandie stepped toward the front door, avoiding the clawed minefield next to her. She inserted the old-fashioned key marked *front* and turned it. *At least she tried.* "Great, perfect. Three hours traveling on a small, smelly bus and now the keys don't work." Her current location, Point Muse, Maine was only three hours away from Andrews, a small college town near Portland. Squeezed in next to a salami-guzzling elderly man wasn't the perfect start to her new life. But here she was, locked out of the only place she now called home.

Theo hissed and Xandie swore he laughed at her. Baring her teeth back, she walked to the end of the porch and peered around the side. There was a gate set into the side of a stone fence. Maybe it led somewhere? The cat meowed as she deserted him. Xandie pushed the gate open and slipped into the back yard, ignoring the murderous feline's high-pitched whine.

"Wow, hope Sera had a gardener." Xandie stared at the lush manicured spread. An old-fashioned stone path wound its way from the gate to the side of the house where a window and a heavy, wood-framed door with ornate carvings gave access to the interior. The path curved back out and down to the middle of the yard where a circular gazebo sat, with several statues dotted around it. Xandie moved toward it, inhaling as she went. The brine of the bay enveloped her senses and a light wind tangled her long brown hair. The house stood on a bluff and looked over the bay and the township of Point Muse.

"And Sera died before I found time to visit her." Xandie shook her head and traced her steps back to the carved door. She wished she'd seen Sera more, but her father disliked his weird aunt. Once her mom had disappeared, he'd wanted nothing to do with Sera again. He blamed her for his wife leaving, disappearing, whatever had happened to her mom. Xandie shook off her melancholy and tried the door. Shut up tight like the front. She looked the bundle of keys over and picked out a dull silver one with the same weird carvings etched into it. She fitted the key, but it refused to turn. Xandie gave up and peered in a window. Dust and brine congealed on the glass, obscuring most of the inside except for a little wooden table and chair in the middle of the room.

"No help there." Xandie headed back to the front of the house and pursed her lips. "Well, monster. How the heck are we getting inside?" Theo growled, and she swore he muttered *useless librarian*. She snickered at her imagination. Xandie had driven her father crazy with the magical worlds and creatures she made up as a child. Every time her mother had taken her for a visit to his aunt, her practical academic father disappeared. Always some important duty interfering with his ability to travel with them. Xandie tried a window at the front of the house and it moved under her hand. "Bingo, cat. We have a winner." She pulled the window open and measured the distance. Thank goodness she was

4

skinny; she should be able to climb in and unlock the door.

She dropped her bag and stooped under the window. With a bunny hop to get her front half in, Xandie gripped the timber frame and hauled herself over, squeaking when her shirt caught on the latch. Stuck halfway in, she leaned toward the floor and tried to wiggle the shirt off the latch, with no success. "I'm jinxed. Someone will find my starved rear end hanging out the window." This time she was positive the cat laughed. She shook a fist at the cat as she hung upside down. "Yeah, it's funny until you realize you're stuck in the damn cage until someone finds my decomposing body." Theo shut up.

"Is the cat your look-out?" A husky male voice came from behind Xandie.

She jerked up and scraped her exposed stomach on the latch of the window. "No, he's the potential murder victim when I get free. Now how about some help?" Heavy steps ambled toward her. From her upside-down position, the only bits visible were men's black shoes and dark pants.

"Well, Miss. I don't think the Police Chief of Point Muse should aid and abet a break-in. Think it's against the law."

Xandie ground her teeth together. *Small town*

idiot policeman. "Who breaks into a house with their cat? And has the keys?" She flapped a hand over her back. "Have a look on the porch. I own this house now. I inherited it when my great-aunt Sera passed away. Now get me the heck out of here." She hissed the last few words.

"This is a classic case of breaking and entering *and* cat napping. I have to call this into my officers."

"Are you freaking kidding me?" Xandie squealed and thumped the window frame. "My purse is in my bag. Check my name out. I'm Xandie Meyers from Andrews, Maine. Sera Meyers was my great-aunt. Now get me free."

The policeman snickered but covered it with a cough. "Ah, this identification has a different name on it."

"Xandie is a nickname. My full name is Alexandra. And why would I take this torturous cat anywhere if I didn't have to? The damn feline hates me to the point of drawing blood." She waved her scored arm in the air to make the point. Who the hell was this idiot?

"Theo clawed you? What did you do to him?" The policeman grabbed Xandie around the waist and freed her shirt from the latch. With a quick tug, he pulled her down and out of the window.

Xandie fell against her rescuer and they both collapsed in a pile of legs and arms. "The cat? I haven't touched him. Mr. Essam, the lawyer, dumped the cage on the porch, threw me the keys and bolted. The animal hates me." She raised her head from the policeman's hard chest and glared at him through the mess of her unruly hair. The man might be a pain in her rear end, but he *was* easy on the eye. Short sandy hair that curled at the ends, laughing blue eyes and a narrow face topped off with a chiseled jaw.

"I can send you a picture."

Shame about his mouth and ego. Xandie growled and shoved herself off the policeman. It was just too bad her bony knees caught him in a painful area. "Not funny. I prefer it if you'd unlock my house. *Before* I make a complaint to your superior." She stomped to the door and stood out of claw zone, waiting.

He rolled to his feet and rubbed his side. "Police Chief Zachery Braun at your service and I *am* my superior." He brushed off his pants and grimaced at her. "Sorry, I ran late and had to field calls about someone breaking into a private residence."

"Oh, I see. Funnier to embarrass and humiliate your newest resident. Perfect." Xandie gritted her teeth and turned her back on the damn man. The whole time he'd known who she was.

"Sorry. It was more amusing when you were upside down." He rubbed his hands through his hair and grabbed the keys from the porch. "Did you try the front door first before you broke in?"

Xandie stomped her foot. She pointed to the door. "I. Am. Not. An. Idiot."

Chief Braun slid the key into the lock and turned it. The door creaked open, and he gestured inside to a gaping Xandie.

"I swear it wouldn't open. The house and the cat hate me." She sagged against the doorframe. Her father might be right. She should sell the house, but Sera had wanted her to stay for a minimum of three months. She'd wanted to see where Sera lived, anyway. *And* find out why her mother had to visit Sera on the day she disappeared. Xandie wanted answers and hoped Point Muse had them.

"Most houses don't have opinions on their owners and Theo wants inside and out of the cage." Braun handed the keys to Xandie as she stormed past.

She stopped in the foyer and stared. The lawyer had explained there were four-bedrooms with two bathrooms, an updated kitchen along with a private library and living room. People came from all over to consult her great-aunt's collection of supernatural and occult texts. Since Xandie had lost her job as a librarian and she'd been stuck working for her dad, this was a godsend of an opportunity. Even if it horrified her staid, academic, librarian father.

Xandie spun around and took in the house. Antique white walls jostled for attention with polished wood floors. The staircase for the upper level swept down and intersected the foyer in the center. Rooms stood off to either side, and she noticed the kitchen behind the staircase. Light poured in from the large front windows and warmed the living room. The house was well worth the delay in getting inside. Xandie lifted her face and closed her eyes for a moment. The hole she hadn't known she had filled with an almost audible click. She was home. Whatever she found out about her mother, even dealing with the cat, it didn't matter. Xandie was home.

"I think your fur baby wants out." Braun carried the cat cage in, nudged Xandie aside and placed it on the floor. He patted the cage then stood and handed her a business card. "Here, call me if you have any problems."

Xandie left him standing with the card

outstretched for as long as she could without looking petty. Then she grabbed the card and let it fall to the table near the entrance. "Thanks for your help. But I'm sure I'll be fine now." She walked toward the Chief, making him walk backward. He stumbled outside onto the porch and Xandie shut the door in his face with a decisive click. *Take that, police chief pain in the bottom.* Xandie rested her back against the door and ignored Theo's loud yowling. She'd made it inside the house and away from that embarrassing man. Caught upside down, entering a house from the window, wasn't the way she wanted to introduce herself to the residents of Point Muse, Maine.

The door behind her back vibrated as someone knocked against it. Seriously? Please don't let it be that annoying Braun man again. She flung the door open and frowned. "I thought you'd left?"

Zachery Braun shoved a bag of cat biscuits and a folder of papers at Xandie. "Thanks for your warm greeting, but I had to give you the cat food. Essam, the lawyer, teed it up with me earlier. Plus, there're papers of Sera's he left outside."

She stuffed her pride down around her knees and mumbled, "Thanks. Sorry. I wanted to get inside."

"If you need me, call." Braun saluted and strode to his car.

Xandie closed the door with care and turned around, hugging the cat food to her chest. *Okay, now she was home.* She dropped the bag on the floor and walked toward the cat cage. Chief Braun had a point. Someone had stuffed the poor animal in a cage for who knows how long. She just hoped he wouldn't take a shot at her once he was free. Grabbing an umbrella with a wooden handle from a stand next to the side table she extended the point until it lay under the cage latch. With a quick push upward, the latch dropped, and the cat shot straight for the kitchen. She hefted the cat food into her arms and followed him. Theo stood near his bowl and meowed pitifully. Xandie filled the food and water container and stood back as the cat wolfed down the food and lapped at the water.

With a sigh, she collapsed onto a kitchen stool and stared out at the garden. She should cut the animal some slack. Sera had died and now he had a stranger for an owner. She'd be annoyed too.

Cat sorted for the moment, Xandie headed toward the front door. The lawyer had dumped her luggage on the side of the porch, and she'd forgotten it in the drama of breaking into the house. She grabbed the bags and dragged them into the hallway near the stairs. She'd carry them up later. For now, she wouldn't mind checking out the house.

Theo padded behind her as she explored. Xandie raced up the stairs and into the bedrooms. Every room was as simple and elegant as the one before. When she reached the master bedroom, Xandie let out a squeal of delight and took a running jump onto the queen-sized bed. Plump, soft blankets surrounded her as she stared up at the romantic four posts around the bed. The whole room screamed Xandie Meyers. Everything she'd ever wanted in a bedroom. A surge of contentment rolled over her and for a moment, Xandie wallowed in it. Then she felt the bay calling her. She scrambled off the bed and headed downstairs again. Theo mumbled and complained behind her as he followed. "Well, you shouldn't eat so much. It's not like I can steal the silver, it's mine. So give me a break."

Xandie dodged the claw and accompanying hiss and covered the stairs at a breakneck speed, desperate to see her whole domain. There were two rooms downstairs, a sitting room and a lounge room/dining room, plus the kitchen and another bathroom. She wandered back through the large, white, pristine kitchen. The furniture fit the house.

Simple, but elegant, even romantic. Perfect for her. From what she'd seen, the clean, functional lines of the house and furniture would've appealed to her great-aunt too.

Xandie remembered a little of Sera from before her father had banned her from visiting. Sera loved to laugh and hug and kiss Xandie. She'd point out every little speck of dust and proclaim the fairies visited. Sera always regaled her with fairy tales and let her ferret around in her library. Theo, much nicer back then, would curl up with her for cuddles and pats. "Now he wants to slice me, piece by piece." Xandie smiled at the thought of her great-aunt's reaction to Theo's nastiness. "She'd have taken your treats away until you played nice."

Theo hissed and took off outside into the garden. Xandie snickered and followed. The back garden was as picture worthy as the house. The white Grecian statues that crowded around a roofed gazebo turned out to be copies of the nine muses. A trellis of colorful flowers covered one side of the building. Leafy trees and shrubs dotted the landscape in groups of two or three, followed by curving flowerbeds interspersed by the old stone path that weaved in and out. An ornamental pond took up one corner of the grounds. The epitome of an English formal garden, only in Maine.

Xandie followed the path and moved closer to the bluff. She found a set of stone stairs and paused for a moment, staring. The steps wound to the beach below. To the right was the bay and the town of Point Muse. At the foot of the stairs, another path led out to the dock and the mooring for an absent boat. Somewhere on the beach, her great-aunt had gone for a swim and never returned. Police found her clothing in a tidy pile, but no Sera until the next day when she washed ashore. With a verdict of accidental drowning, the council and the police department closed the case. Xandie shivered and stared out over the bay. So calm and inviting. The water didn't look like a murderer at all.

She turned to stare at the house. *Her house.* She followed another path that led straight up to the side door she'd tried earlier. Diverting from the walkway, she stood in front of a window that faced the bay and peered inside. Xandie remembered playing and snoozing in the library, taking it all in as Sera made up wonderful stories about the magical people who lived in Point Muse. The tales had kept a little girl entertained for hours.

Xandie remembered combing the house for

fairies and pretending a stray dog was a vicious were-wolf. Her father had shattered her daydreams once she arrived home and declared everything his aunt had told her was nonsense. She grimaced. Her father considered facts to be an important foundation for a growing girl. He outlawed fiction and fairytales. Especially once her mother disappeared. Shaking off her maudlin thoughts, Xandie focused on the window in front of her. She peered in.

The interior looked dusty but inviting. Light from the window showed off row after row of shelves lined with bound books. A heavy carved reading desk and chair sat in the middle of the room with various small chairs and tables dotted around. Books and papers covered every available inch of space. Floors, chairs, desk and shelves covered with pages of knowledge and learning. She couldn't wait to get in there and tidy. *Once a librarian, always a librarian.* In fact, it was the family business. Her father, Russell Meyers, had informed her every family member in the past had a working attachment to a library and books. The same obsession passed through the line to her.

Theo hissed and swiped at her legs while she drooled over the library. Cursing, Xandie spun around and tried to catch Theo as he ran back into the house. "I hope you spew all your lovely food up. And don't think I'm cleaning up after you." She started to follow the cat but stopped when she spotted someone in dark clothing dart from the bushes to the front of property. Xandie ran inside to the kitchen, but the figure had disappeared. Why trespass? Maybe they'd wanted a look-see, a teenager wanting to see where someone had died? She scanned the kitchen, but nothing seemed out of place except for a hissing Theo who jumped up and knocked over the police chief's paperwork.

Xandie gathered the papers and hissed when her finger pricked on a sharp point. Sucking the blood off her pinkie, she stared at a simple necklace with a pendent in the shape of a sun with an eye etched onto the gold. *Sera's necklace.* She'd worn it every day. Called it her good luck charm. Had she taken it off to go for a swim? Xandie guessed it belonged to her now. She attached the necklace around her neck and piled the paperwork back on the bench.

Theo mewled and brushed against her leg. "Now you approve of me? A cat who likes gold?" Xandie reached out and ran a hand along his spine. Theo arched and purred. *Fickle animal.* She straightened and made sure she'd locked the kitchen door behind her. Her great-aunt's death might have been accidental, but Xandie was still a stranger in a strange town. Didn't hurt to be careful. And speaking of Point Muse, she had to grab supplies before she was reduced to eating Theo's cat biscuits.

Neither one of them would survive that.

TWO

Her bottom may never recover. Xandie adjusted her seat on Sera's bicycle. Someone needed to design extra padding, because after this ride she wasn't sitting anytime soon. If she hadn't had a meeting with the agent who'd looked after Sera's estate, Xandie would've avoided the bike like the plague. Exercise wasn't her thing. But the woman had rung late last night, adamant she had to speak with Xandie. So here she was, cruising Main Street, Point Muse, and taking in the sights.

The town had a mix of wood and brick buildings, with an abundance of gables, cute porches and bay windows. She'd also passed Mayweather Inn, near to Sera's house. Now she was closing in on the joint council chambers and small police department.

"Thanks to Chief Braun, I've no interest in drop-ping in for a chat with the local cop." Xandie sniffed and concentrated on peddling. Okay, she may have been a tad grumpy, but you get defensive when made fun of. She slowed to a crawl to take in the charm of the small town. A group of people gathered near the real estate agent's door distracted Xandie and she tilted. She directed her bike to the side of the street before a car took her out. *At least Theo stayed at home, otherwise he'd be roadkill the way I'm handling this bicycle.*

"Watch out."

Xandie froze at the barked comment and touched her brakes. An older man jumped out of the way and she crashed into the ornate metal fence out the front of the real estate agency. Xandie winced as she scraped her leg. "Ouch." She slid off the bike, resting it against the fence. The throng of people near the door shifted but were too engrossed peering through the agent's windows to pay attention to her clumsiness.

"You're a danger on that contraption. I told Sera she needed to buy a scooter." The older gentleman frowned at the bicycle before switching his disap-proving gaze to Xandie.

Xandie held her hands up in defense. "You were in the middle of the street."

"I was crossing. It's not like we have traffic jams here. I assumed you'd notice me and adjust your course."

Okay, she'd possibly been sightseeing too much while riding the wretched bike. "I'm sorry. Were you hurt?" God help her if he wanted to complain to Braun. He'd have a field day.

"No, I'm fine. Apologies for yelling, it was a shock." He gestured to her leg. "I think you're the one hurt. Do you need help?"

Xandie peered at her leg, but since she'd worn jeans and to look at it she'd have to strip in Main Street, she was going with fine with a side of painful limping. At least, until she got home and inspected the damage. "It's tender."

"Maybe you should take a seat? You must be still adjusting to your great-aunt's death."

"I'm fine. Did everyone know my aunt Sera?"

The older man smirked. "Occupational hazard for a small town." He extended his hand. "I'm Professor Amoru. Here on a working vacation. I knew your aunt through her library. Will you continue her work?"

Way to pin her to the spot. Xandie forced a smile

and shook his hand. She winced when her necklace tightened around her neck. *Must have caught on something.* She tugged it away and rubbed her neck. "Not sure what I'm doing for the moment. I only arrived yesterday."

"I've petitioned Sera for access to her reference materials. I'm positive she was granting it. Can I still count on your approval for access?"

His eyes flashed red for a moment and Xandie took a step back. Trick of the light? She focused on his words. "I'll assess your paperwork and decide my course of action. You must have Sera's home number? Call me in a few days. I should be up to speed by then."

"That's fine. No rush. All the time in the world." He smiled and raised a hand in farewell as he navigated back across the road.

"Okay, strange. But I guess we aren't in the city anymore." Xandie checked her watch. She might as well head to her appointment, provided she could get past the crowd without inciting a riot. She pushed up to the front, apologizing, "Excuse me. Sorry. I have a meeting."

An older lady snorted and tapped on the door. "Not with her you don't."

"Aren't Point Muse residents known for their

friendliness?" Xandie tried the handle, but it was locked.

"Only when they want." The other lady brushed her pink-dyed hair away from around her chubby face. "And I wasn't rude. Workmen found a body, we think its Louise Maker, the agent."

"Oh, okay. I guess there's no meeting then." The agent had died? She'd only spoken to her last night. Xandie shivered. *Welcome to Point Muse.*

"Who did you say you were?"

"I didn't. But I'm Xandie Meyers. Sera was my great-aunt."

Pink-haired lady nodded. "Sera's little niece. She talked about you."

"Did she?" Xandie hadn't seen Sera in years.

"Yes, she came in as regular as clockwork for her rinse until she died. Sad to hear she's gone, but glad you're home now. We look forward to seeing you soon."

"Rinse? A few days?" Xandie shook her head. "I'm still playing catch up."

"We did Sera's hair. But we saw her every month for our meetings." She pointed at the hairdressing salon on the opposite side. "*Hair Today Gone Tomorrow* is our place."

Another lady with a matching purple coif

nodded. "Of course, dear, we're eager to look at your follicles. But my sister-in-law's referring to the soon-to-be-held ceremony at your property in a few days. Don't you worry, it's all in under control, the mayor will be in contact with you to confirm. Now we must be going." She dragged her sister-in-law back across the street and into a pastel-fronted building.

Xandie peered in the agent's door, but a group of dark-shirted men blocked whatever lay on the floor. Paint tins sat in one corner and a half-plastered wall in the other. *If they were working on the office, why arrange a meeting there?* Another figure moved into view and squatted. Police chief on the scene. She'd recognize those large black shoes anywhere. She shuffled away from the group. All he had to do was read the appointment book and he'd realize the agent was scheduled to see Xandie this morning. Braun would be on her case soon so she might as well be comfy when he interrogated her. She peered along the street and spotted a cute bakery close by. Ignoring the bike, she limped toward sugary heaven. Anyone who wanted the stupid machine could have the cursed thing. She was using her own two feet from here on out.

The bakery had a lovely painted sign over the store titled *'Heart's Delight'* and ornate white tables and chairs on the front porch. She pushed open the door and stopped. A stone fireplace dominated the room; real old-fashioned hearth that come winter would pump out heat. Tables and booths along with comfy chairs dotted the room and a glass cabinet filled with pastries of goodness drew her.

"What's your poison?"

Wha? Xandie opened her eyes wide. "Whatever the agent didn't buy this morning."

The server smirked, then reassembled her expression into something more business-like one. "Anything catch your fancy? The blueberry sour cream coffee cake is great, or cinnamon butter puffs, shortbread cookies, bagels?"

Sugar. Xandie's resistance to calories melted away at the sound of a butter puff. "I'll grab a puff and a hot chocolate."

"Busting out the sugar today. Overdose it is."

Xandie wandered over to a seat next to the window. Prime viewing position for when Braun stalked her down.

"Here we go." The woman handed Xandie her food and went back for the drink.

She nibbled at the puff. Her eyes rolled back as the spiced sugar hit her taste buds. She mumbled her appreciation and kept eating.

"Our best sellers." The server slid the drink onto the table and plunked herself opposite. "How you enjoying our town so far?"

Swallowing the delicious mouthful, Xandie focused on the person in front of her. A tall, curvy girl with mischief-filled amber eyes and brown hair in a wave of curls. "Everyone knows I inherited Sera's home?"

"Yep, no secrets here. Especially when fresh blood comes into our strange little town."

"Strange is the keyword. So far, I've met an annoying policeman, a runaway lawyer and two colorful-haired ladies who want to get hold of my follicles."

"Oh, that's nothing. Wait until you deal with the witches, bears, wolves, trolls and assorted weird and wacky characters that populate Point Muse. I'm Lila Harrow. Resident baker and owner of *Heart's Delight* and a descendent of the original earth witch, Elizabeth Harrow." She bobbed her head in a gracious introduction.

Xandie snickered. That spiel sounded familiar. "Sera made up Point Muse stories. I loved it as a kid. I'd spend hours hoping to find a fairy ring or an ogre or two. The town has adopted the theme to encourage tourism, I guess."

Lila frowned. "Ah, no I'm serious. I'm descended from an earth witch. Didn't Sera ever explain?"

"I hardly saw her while growing up and once my mom disappeared, Dad refused to let me visit." She hunched over her mug and sipped the chocolate froth. There may be more to this town than her father or her great-aunt had ever explained.

"I forgot about your mom. But Point Muse isn't a fairy-tale. Things that go bump in the night here actually bump or bite back."

Was everyone crazy here? For once in her life she had no words. But in the back of Xandie's mind she had a weird feeling of déjà vu. Lila and Sera's tales might not be so outlandish.

Lila patted her on the back. "Don't worry, sweetie. Once you get into the library Sera will explain everything. But listen to Theo too. He won't steer you wrong."

"The cat?" *And how was a dead woman supposed to explain?* Xandie rubbed her forehead. A migraine was brewing.

"I'm always here if you need to download the craziness that is Point Muse. Plus, Chief Hottie is after you." Lila pointed out the window as the police officer stomped his way into the bakery.

Chief pain in the bottom. Xandie grimaced and

shoveled the last of her butter puff in her mouth. He wasn't ruining her taste of heaven in a puff.

"I hear you were in a vehicular accident and you had a meeting with a dead person. Congrats on a day well done." Braun collapsed onto Lila's abandoned chair and glared straight at Xandie. "What do you do for an encore?"

"Drink my hot chocolate in peace?"

"Why did you meet with Louise Maker?"

She moved her drink out of throwing reach. Food and drink this good shouldn't be wasted on a painful law enforcement officer. "Let's be clear. She called me to schedule a meeting. I turned up, and you were already there. In fact, I have a pile of witnesses with rainbow-dyed hair who'll swear I never entered the building. Check the hairdressers if you need statements."

He shuddered. "My momma cuts my hair. Those old women would eat me alive if I stepped in there. I'll take your word for it."

"Any idea what happened to the woman? She wouldn't explain what she wanted to discuss. Just that it was important."

"The coroner decides cause of death. When did she call you?"

"Around ten last night." The woman had been

27

pushy and a tad anxious, but otherwise harmless. Surely the death was accidental? "Did she trip and hit her head or have a heart attack?"

Braun shook his head. "I can't say much, but it doesn't look like an accident and someone overheard her at the Inn bar talking up a big deal. I'm assuming she thought you'd sell Sera's house to her."

What? "Terms of the will. I stay in the place for three months before I can sell, and I haven't decided I want to, anyway. I've only been here twenty-four hours." She played with her drink. "If it wasn't an accident, and she was excited about a nonexistent sale, it wasn't suicide. Someone killed her?"

"Look," he leaned forward on his elbows and lowered his voice, "it'll get around town, anyway. We found her electrocuted. The coffee pot had intentionally frayed cords; she'd only just bought the pot. Maker filled it up and water must have got on the cord or she had wet hands. Who knows? But we found burn marks on both hands and a contusion on the side of her head. We hoped her appointment book might give us more insight, but since you've an alibi, obviously not. We've no clue why she was even there. The mayor's secretary warned her not to use the points until they installed the new safety circuits."

"Secretary?"

"Irene Cummings. She's the mayor's sister and personal assistant. Cummings owns the deceased's office building." He pushed himself away from the table. "Be careful and take things easy while you slide into town life. Point Muse isn't for the weak of heart." He nodded to Lila and swung out without a backward glance.

"Am I a suspect?" Xandie appealed to Lila as she sidled up. First Zach Braun made fun of her and now interrogation. She had no clue what to think of him.

"Honey, you're what we'd call a person of interest. In fact, everyone in town's curious. We're waiting to see your next move." Lila winked at Xandie.

Xandie dropped her head to the table and contemplated the worn tabletop. "Hopefully it isn't another dead body." Weren't small towns supposed to be peaceful? There might be more to Sera leaving her the estate than just a plain old inheritance.

"Time will tell, sweetie. Time will tell."

THREE

"Listen to the cat she says." Xandie held Theo up to her face and scrunched her nose. "I'm listening. Speak, revered feline." Theo mewled and licked her nose. Xandie giggled and set him down on the floor. "This whole town is crazy. She wants me to go into the library and speak to my dead great-aunt and listen to a cat. Funny, she seemed nice and sane before that comment."

Shrugging, she tightened her fingers around the key to the library door. "This time the key will work, and no funny business will happen. I will *not* see a body or the ghost of Sera." When Xandie was younger, she remembered her aunt swore the library was alive. It chose the information to give and who to enter. When Xandie napped in the large chairs, sometimes it seemed as if the library talked to her, whispering stories of the supernatural world and its inhabitants.

She snorted. "I should be a writer with that kind of imagination." But she still placed an ear against the door, listening for any weird and wacky voices. All she heard was the damn cat sniggering behind her back.

"Right, ignore me." She pushed the key into the lock and turned it. The movement was smooth, ending with a gratifying click, the sticky lock from move-in day a thing of the past. The door swung open, and she stumbled into the receiving room. "Sera always said you had to receive the visitors first to make sure they were right for the library. She'd either let them in or get the information herself."

Funny, no one had been in here for a while and she'd locked the door, so where did all the dust go? She swiped her hand over the small table that sat in the middle of the room...clean. Disturbed, Xandie backed away and turned to the internal door. Solid as a bank vault. She thumped her hand against it. Heavy dark wood greeted her touch. It would require an army to take the door out.

Xandie gasped as the portal swung open with no effort on her part. After a few breaths to settle the wild thumping of her heart, she leaned forward to take a quick peek. When she'd peered through the windows yesterday, everything had looked unloved and dusty. Now the shelves and tables gleamed, not a speck of dirt in sight.

Not knowing what to expect, she took a few cautious steps into the room, Theo curling around her feet and purring as she did. Light from the beautiful big picture window sparkled and reflected off the polished tables placed around the room. At least, those parts not covered in papers and books. A lovely carved desk placed in the center of the room had a large high-backed chair next to it. This too hosted a stack of paperwork and discarded books. "Looks like a throne for a librarian queen, doesn't it, Theo?" He mewled an agreement and jumped up to groom himself. "Or a king, I guess." Snickering, Xandie traced a hand over the gold-embossed spine of the nearest book. She shivered and leaned over and sniffed. Nothing like the musty smell of knowledge. She laughed at herself. What could be better than walking into your own floor-to-ceiling library. Not to mention, one whole wall dedicated to ancient scrolls.

"Father would love this place if it wasn't in Point Muse." She made a note to call him when she finished her inventory of the library. He'd left messages for the last twenty-four hours since she'd arrived, and she was currently dodging him. Xandie tired of his lectures of what she should do and selling Sera's house was top of the list for her father. Top of *her* list, though, was putting things away and cleaning up. It looked like a tornado had whirled through the library. "A librarian's job is never finished, hey, mouser?" Xandie smiled at Theo and rubbed her hands in glee. Time to get to it.

She peered at the shelves and tried to find an order to how Sera shelved her books. Neither Library of Congress nor Dewey decimal system were used. Instead, she'd grouped everything according to her own classification. "Simple, I guess. Shifters in one group, bears/berserkers, cat, croc, rabbit, hyena, nagual and assorted other groups." Xandie quirked an eyebrow. *Shifters?* She scanned another shelf. This one was animals turning into humans, next one was varieties of vampires. Vampire, dhampir, draugr, byronic vampires, penangglan, strigoi and nachzeher. *"Say what?"*

Xandie strode to the other side of the room and ran her fingers along another shelf. "Species of fairies. Ashray, avaoln, ballyblog, banshee, brownie, changeling, clurichaun." She squatted down and read the bottom shelves. "Lists of demons who have visited the earthly plane. Abaddon, abraxas, ahriman, aim, amdusisa, amon." She stood and drifted around in a circle. Every book here was about supernatural creatures and occurrences. Who would be interested in that kind of reference material?

Theo mewled and pawed at the papers on the desk. Rushing to stop him damaging anything precious, Xandie accidentally bumped a scroll off the desk. She picked it up and unrolled it, her curiosity getting the better of her. At first the lettering looked like ancient Greek, but the words jumbled and reformed into English. She closed her eyes for a moment, opened them again. *Yep, still English.* But she'd have sworn they were in another language to start with. This scroll was an account of the sacking and burning of the Great Library of Alexandria by the demonic roman, Julius Caesar. Authored by an unnamed librarian. "Demonic?" Xandie queried Theo, surprised when he hissed and his fur stood on end. "Okay, you aren't a fan of Julius Caesar." She rolled the scroll up and continued to shelve books and scrolls away according to their content.

A few hours later Xandie stretched her back and moaned. For such a small space, who would have thought it contained so much information and could get in such a mess? Theo licked himself, slept and hissed at anything to do with Julius Caesar while she worked. At least the room was clean again. She'd gone back to the basics of library work and shelved, back in touch with her roots. To be honest, the work was interesting too. She'd had no clue how many species of shifter and venomous sentient plants there were. That's if she believed in the supernatural. Xandie frowned for a moment. But the words written were plausible and backed up by multiple sources. And a large part of her screamed Sera wasn't crazy, and this was *her* life now.

There was even a shelf for Templar Knights who'd fought for and against different supernatural groups. She'd found a scroll on the Knights Sanguis, a violent splinter offshoot of the Templars. The knights of Pure Blood had sworn to track down impure humans and creatures and slaughter them to protect pure human bloodlines. Xandie shook her head and placed the scroll back on the shelf. There'd even been knights attached to Hitler. That's why the information was so interesting because it was fact based. Maybe Sera's tales of Point Muse weren't crazy.

The library was all-quiet except for the light snoring of Theo in the great chair. So when the phone rang from the welcome room, Xandie jerked in shock and bumped a shelf, dodging the avalanche of books that toppled. She growled at the small pile of books and moved to answer the phone. This was the first time she'd heard a phone ring in the house at all. "Yes?"

An officious female voice replied. "Miss Alexandra Meyers?"

"Xandie. How can I help you?"

"This is Irene Cummings, calling for Mayor Nigel Cummings. He'd like to arrange lunch up at the Inn with you to talk about the anniversary celebrations on Friday."

"That's only twenty-four hours away." Anniversary? What did it have to do with her?

"Yes, he will inform you of your requirements. Meet him at the Inn by twelve thirty promptly." The woman hung up without waiting for an answer.

Xandie stared at the phone. Officious or what? She peeped at her watch. She still had a little while before she needed to get ready for her first social outing in Point Muse. At least she had the time to fix the mess she'd knocked over. She dropped the phone and walked back to the books, shelving them away. This section was all about disappearances in and around Point Muse. She stopped for a moment and picked up a ledger.

Flicking it open, she scanned a page. "Wow." There were a surprising number of names on the list, spanning over a hundred years. One name shocked the pants off her. Her mother, Miranda Meyers. It listed the date she disappeared, the circumstances and her connection to Point Muse and to the Harrows through birth. "Harrow? That's Lila's last name." Her mom had a link to Point Muse she had no clue about. Her father always insisted her mom had no family.

She needed to call him, but right now she had to get ready. Xandie dropped the book on the big desk, intending to come back and study it later. As she did a slip of paper fell out.

"Great. More surprises." But this time Theo meowed and nudged it toward her. "Fine for you, mouser. But I better not find a secret twin sister." Xandie opened it and realized it was a letter. She read it aloud to Theo.

Dearest Xandie,

I'm guessing right about now you're cursing me for keeping secrets from you. You should. If it had been up to me, you'd have known your heritage from the beginning. But your father never believed and was stubborn enough to ignore everything right under his nose.

Our family line is a long and proud one. We can date our line back to Demetrius of Phaleron. The scholar who founded the Great Library of Alexandria. Our family has always been librarians, scribes and scholars. Anything to do with books and knowledge, our family was in the thick of it. We served the Great Library in whatever function it required. People came from all over the world to consult the Library. But little did the known world realize what hid within. There has always been another world within the human one. The world I tried to tell you in stories and fairy tales. A world that had bear shifters and werewolves, fairies and demons. It exists, and the hidden core function of the Great library has always contained knowledge of the supernatural world and its inhabitants.

The library hid her core in plain sight. Shelves of human knowledge camouflaging its real treasures. But with treasure comes treasure hunters. The library is a sentient. The how of her making is lost to the ages and Demetrius always refused to answer on the process. But the Library chooses who accessed her and what information to share.

One such treasure seeker came calling but was

refused entrance. Unknown to other humans, an old demonic entity possessed the man. He became obsessed with gaining entrance to all supernatural knowledge to destroy his enemies. This man sacked Alexandria and burned the library. His name was Julius Caesar, and the demon within named Amon. The library knew this and took action to preserve herself. As long as our line is still alive in the outside world, she could tie herself to our energy and give away her physical form.

We directed the information allowed to us by the library. While the demon attacked the library a young man of our line was studying within. The library transformed Theon into the avatar or guardian. A bridge between our line and the library. A guide. Although he can be annoying. The necklace you are hopefully wearing proclaims you a librarian of the great library. The library and Theo will show you how everything works.

Above all, watch out for the demon Amon. He still craves access although he can be a charmer when he wants to be and oddly honorable. But still watch for him. Be on guard. Other people and organizations would love to control the library and will stop at nothing to achieve that. Pure blood is an evil obsession and will bring down the world. If the library falls, so do the people who depend on it.

I love you, sweetie, and wish I could be there to see you, but the library has warned that someone is hunting me. I write this letter to prepare you.

Stay safe.
Sera.

Either her aunt was insane or the weird and wacky supernatural creatures she spun a tale about lived.

And what did Sera mean about open her ears and eyes? A stray whisper of noise behind Xandie caught her attention. She spun, but nothing was there, not even Theo the cat who'd wandered off. She concentrated again on the letter. She had a feeling the library, and her inheritance, weren't the windfalls she'd thought them to be.

This time the whispers became louder from another corner of the library. Xandie froze and faced the noises that were now green lights that flickered and glowed. They scooted over every inch of space, every shelf, every book, every scroll. Even dancing over Xandie herself, tickling her with little green glowing touches. The lights centered on her necklace, growing until they formed a green lace pattern around her neck and shoulders. Around Sera's necklace. The link between the library and her family. The glow faded, but the whispers grew. She heard them now, whispering of strange mysteries and people. Whispering its knowledge to her. She winced as the noise grew louder and louder. Now chanting one word over and over.

Blood.

Blood.

Blood.

"Enough," Xandie yelled, hands over her ears as she backed up against the door. "My ears can't handle the noise. One at a time." The whispers withdrew until one lingered and whispered once more.

Blood.

She sagged back against the door. "Way to blow my ordinary mind." Everything was true, and the library was alive and that meant someone might be after it. What had the library meant about blood? Did it mean Sera's death wasn't an accident? Or was it talking about something else? Frustrated, Xandie let herself out of the library, hands shaking. Too many unanswered questions bubbled in her mind.

Her little world had exploded into a universe of

unknown. She checked her watch, but everything had to wait. Because as of now, she was late for the mayor's meeting and judging by the past few hours, it might end up an interesting lunch.

Mayweather Inn was the place to have secret meetings or an illicit tryst. Xandie rested Sera's old silver bike against the side of the building and drank in the Inn. Victorian style with sweeping lines and white gables. Round columns soared into the air, and a pretty picket fence and a sweet-smelling rose trellis completed the picture.

Xandie swept up the stairs like a debutante going to the ball...in her jeans. She tugged at them self-consciously as she entered the formal entranceway. She'd ditched her formal library wear as soon as she left Andrews College and her father. An ageing lady with pink cheeks and a frilly nineteen fifties style skirt and top greeted her.

"You must be Xandie. It's good to meet you." The woman drew Xandie in for a stale perfume hug.

"Ah, great. Thank you." Xandie had no clue who the woman was, but she didn't think the woman had been a friend of her great-aunt's. The coiffed housewife image wouldn't have appealed to Sera, but who knew what her great-aunt liked? Sera had been a woman of contradictions.

The other woman trilled a fake laugh. "Oh, my goodness, aren't I silly? I'm Rose Mayweather and I own the Inn. I knew your great-aunt Sera." The woman's smile flickered. "I can't claim to be her best friend, but we had a cordial detente. Until she stole my man. But you don't want to hear about that." Rose patted Xandie on the arm and grimaced when she spotted Xandie's jeans. "I'm sure Mayor Cummings won't mind what you're wearing. He's such a lovely man."

Wow, Sera must have hated this woman. If it's the one thing she remembered about great-aunt Sera, it was her lack of domestication. A housewife she was not. Xandie noticed her surroundings as Rose led the way to the dining room. Laughter and yelling drifted from behind a closed door and she'd bet her last dollar that was the bar.

The dining room comprised a mass of heavy chairs and tables with white linen cloths and pretty vases all sat in the center of the room with a dance floor off to the side. Bay windows and seating at the front of the room completed the picture. Burgundy carpet graced the floor and light-colored wood-paneled walls gave an old-world feel to the room. The whole atmosphere was that of a genteel men's club with dim lighting, even with the windows. Xandie snickered, the bakery was more her pace.

"Right here, sweetie." Rose grabbed a chair and pushed Xandie into it. "The mayor is in the bar pressing the flesh, so to speak. He's up for re-election soon."

Xandie laughed, covering it by coughing into her hand before smiling at Rose. "Thank you, Mrs. Mayweather."

"Rose, honey. Now can I get you a drink?"

"A glass of water."

Rose winked. "Hitting the hard stuff there. Water coming up."

Xandie tapped the table. She suspected the Mayor would hit her with this anniversary ceremony. It was the last thing she needed. She had to learn the whole library gig and deal with a supposed talking cat. But agreeing to the ceremony might collect good-will points from Point Muse residents. And that might be a smart idea since she didn't understand the conflict between Sera and the town. Rose hadn't like Sera. Who knew what other enemies her great-aunt might have had? Not to mention, someone here might have known her mom or her family. Something else to put on her to-do list. Stalk missing mother's mysterious family.

"This lovely young lady at my table has to be Alexandra Meyers." The mayor stopped next to the table with a quirky smile and extended a well-manicured hand.

She nodded and shook his hand. His nails were neater than hers. She had a habit of gnawing on hers when she was nervous. "Correct, Mr. Mayor, but please, Xandie, not Alexandra."

He seated himself down and turned the wattage of his smile up on Xandie. "In that case, it's Nigel, lovely lady. It's fantastic to meet you. Sera used to rave about her favorite great-niece."

Xandie snorted. "The only great-niece, but it's still nice to know. I didn't get to visit much when I was a child."

He nodded and patted her hand in fake comfort. "Yes, your mother disappearing must have been a devastating. But you're here now and Point Muse will be better for it."

She nodded and flashed a polite smile while reading the menu. The mayor appeared to be in his late forties or early fifties with light blonde hair crafted to hide his receding hairline. He wasn't bad looking, but everything seemed forced like he was on the campaign trail twenty-four seven. All she needed to know was what he wanted her to do, then she could head home to her library.

Rose popped up and rubbed the mayor's shoulders. "Nice to see little Xandie here in Point Muse and in Sera's house. No offense to your great-aunt, Xandie, but she was sometimes a tad abrasive."

Yep. No love lost between those two.

"Now, now. Claws back in, Rosie." Nigel Cummings smiled and shrugged. "Rosie and Sera clashed a little, but it's all worked out now."

Yeah, her aunt died. Xandie scanned the menu for the quickest and fastest meal possible.

"Now, what can I get you?"

"Something light. Your Greek salad sounds great."

Rose dropped a hand and her smile slipped a little as she wrote the order down.

Nigel shook his head. "Liquid lunch for me. Irene is doing a big cook up tonight; she won't be impressed if I pass."

Rose nodded and left with the order.

The Mayor leaned forward with a serious expression in place on his face. "Sera's death saddened everyone. But she kept herself apart from the town. Credit to her though, she gave one hundred and ten percent when asked." He paused and waited for Xandie to speak.

Oh yeah, he wanted something. "Sound's great, Nigel." Xandie shuddered a little inside as she used his first name.

"Before she passed away, Sera offered her garden for the ceremony of Point Muse's anniversary founding." He paused and smiled at Rose as she settled Xandie's food in front of her.

"The planning's completed. But we need your approval for the use of the land tomorrow night."

And there it was. At least she'd already had a heads up about tomorrow. Not much Xandie could do but smile and agree. "Sound's fine. I'm more than happy for the ceremony to go ahead. But I need to know what to do."

"Great news and you don't need to do anything. Irene has it all planned. She'll organize the troops. My sister has the soul of a general. You just have to open the house and the grounds."

Xandie forked a mouthful of green leaves into her mouth and nodded. Hopefully that was all he needed from her.

Mayor Cummings lowered his voice. "Even with Sera agreeing, we weren't sure the ceremony would go ahead because of the development."

She masterfully swallowed her bitter salad. "Development?"

"An outside company bought the land next to Sera's property. They plan to develop a large spa resort and country club. Your great-aunt's land with a private beach and mooring would be an added attraction to their proposed clientele."

Hell no. No way Sera would have agreed to that and Xandie wouldn't either. Talk about spoiling peace and serenity.

The mayor agreed with Xandie's unspoken words. "No, Sera wasn't interested when they approached her. The company even had executives fly down to ask her and Sera wouldn't budge or even open the door."

"When? Sera never spoke about a development in her sporadic emails."

"The week before she died." He leaned in. "I half expected locals to form a secret lynching party to oust Sera. But then she died, and you inherited. The secret ploy was useless in the long run. Smart, but useless."

Wow, lynching party. How much did people hate Sera here? "Secret ploy?"

"Well, it's common knowledge land owned on the

bluff in theory reverts to town holdings if the owner dies without a beneficiary. A long-standing by-law. But your lawyer Neville Essam informed the Council Sera had made a new will naming you the heir."

Had someone wanted the land bad enough to knock Sera off? "Is the by-law common knowledge? Point Muse is a small town. Wouldn't Sera's new will make the gossip rounds?"

The mayor shook his head. "Everyone knows about the by-law, but Sera only made her will the same day she died. The gossip didn't have time to get around."

Someone might have thought knocking Sera off was a good way to get her land or was the library the reason Sera had to go?

"The library here in Point Muse is important to the lifeblood of our town. So of course, Sera as the librarian had to be here in Point Muse, same as you now." The mayor winked and downed his beer in one long gulp. "As long as you stick to the guidelines laid out in the will and the council by-laws you have nothing to worry about. I'm sure your lawyer, Neville, filled you in." He stood and with a practiced smile took Xandie's hand in a too-tight grip. "Things to do. Nice meeting you, Xandie. I'm sure you'll be easier to work with once you understand the lay of the land."

Xandie smiled weakly and surreptitiously wiped her hand on her leg. Politicians make sweaty handshakers.

He threw money on the table. "I'm sure you won't mind fixing your own tab. Mustn't make a case for council bribery." And he left without a backward glance.

Xandie shoved her plate aside and flicked her own money on the table. "Talk about a cheapskate," she muttered to herself. But with her words came a shiver of worry along her spine. Someone may have murdered Sera for her land or the library, but who knew which? She had to ferret out the truth. Xandie owned the library *and* the land now and she might be a target herself.

Maybe Lila would help with finding information. Plus, the friendly bakery owner might know about Xandie's mother. She pushed away from the table, searching for the bathroom. Spotting a discrete door off the side of the dining room, she weaved her way through the tables toward it.

Something else Mayor Cummings had mentioned stuck in a head. He was certain her lawyer had told her about any will or council requirements for her inheritance. She nibbled her lip as she pushed the door open, not bothering to read the writing plastered on the front. All her lawyer had mentioned was that she had to live in the house for three months and couldn't sell during that period. Now she was worried there were more things he hadn't told her.

She barely noticed her surroundings until a shrill squeak cut her meandering short.

"Staff, office staff. Can't you read?" Rose Mayweather stuffed her shirt back into her skirt waistband. She patted her hair back into place and cleared her throat. "Thank you for paying your tab, Aaron. The Mayweather Inn looks forward to more of your business."

A redhead brute of a man with battering rams for shoulders stepped out from behind Rose's cluttered desk. "Give it a rest, Rosie. She's not as stupid as she looks."

Did he call her stupid? She wasn't the one making out behind an unlocked door. "I was looking for the bathroom before I leave. I saw nothing." Xandie backed away from the couple with her hands raised in apology. She'd definitely caused an interruptus, judging by Rose's air of frustration and the guy's grumpy comment.

Rose looked surprised. "Oh, you're finished with the mayor already? By the way he stalked Sera, I thought he'd keep you at the table for longer. He always liked to take his time." Aaron shot Rosie the evil eye. Flustered, she ignored him and kept talking. "Lunch, I mean. He likes to take a while to eat."

Huh? "He spent time with Sera?"

Rose snorted. "No, he chased her. People around here always wanted something from her and that damn house. She'd get visitors calling at all hours and never say a word about it to anyone the next day. But I guess that's the work of a librarian to The Great Library, isn't it?" Rose drew herself up. "Even that fancy Professor couldn't get enough of her. I must admit, I thought he might be different, but I saw him and Sera squabbling with each other outside the hairdresser. She made it clear he would never step one foot inside her house while she lived. He kept pushing her until she stormed off. The next week she was dead, and I suppose it didn't matter anymore."

The mayor and Professor Amoru? They had both chased after Sera, but was it her great-aunt or the library?

"That stuff doesn't matter. What does, is that she keeps her trap shut about what she didn't see." Aaron loomed over Xandie, causing her to back away. "You hear me? If it gets around, I'll know who the big mouth is."

Xandie zipped her fingers across her mouth and scooted out the door, hearing Rose grumbling in the background as she left.

"Oh, Aaron, honey. Calm down. Who'd believe her, anyway?"

What's the bet Aaron honey had a not-so-sweet wife? The last thing Xandie wanted to do was gossip about anyone. She just needed to get back to her green glowing library and peace from the devious doings of Point Muse.

Whoever said small towns were calm had never lived in Point Muse.

FOUR

Theo's snickering woke Xandie from her demented dream of chocolate-dipped handcuffs and Police Chief Braun. With a groan, she rolled over and buried her head in the blankets. She needed to erase the image from her stressed-out mind. She opened an eye. "You couldn't wake me earlier? Before I dreamed of chocolate and that man?"

Theo sniffed and pawed at the window, meowing.

"Seriously? You need to go out now?" She huffed hair out of her face and searched for her phone. "Two in the morning? Are you kidding me? Can't you use kitty litter?"

Theo growled and curled his upper lip back.

"Fine." Xandie stumbled out of bed and pulled

on a thick sweater over her short pajamas. Thankfully, it wasn't winter yet. But it still got chilly when you only wore skimpy little pajamas. She peeped outside and froze when she saw a flickering light in the garden. "Guess you didn't need a pee trip. You might make a guard dog yet." She patted the cat on his head, avoiding his outstretched claws, and snuck downstairs holding her phone. Who knows if it would even work though. A fact she'd learned about Point Muse is that coverage was spotty. Some days you held your breath and hoped for the best.

Braun had given her his number, but she never thought she'd have to use it and it was his private number too, *score for her*. She dialed, but the call went straight to message bank. "Xandie Meyers here. Spotted lights in my backyard. I think someone's here." She disconnected without a goodbye and snuck through the kitchen door to outside. At least the call had gone through. She turned on her phone's torch app, hand shading it so only a small circle of illumination showed at her feet. It wouldn't do to let her intruder know she was onto him—or her.

If it had been Sera, she could have walked outside blindfolded. Xandie hadn't lived here long enough to memorize the backyard. She followed the bobbing lights to the side of the property, furthest away from the road.

She dropped to her knees and crawled until she found a large bushy tree to hide behind. Then she peered out. She was wrong. There wasn't one light, but six. In fact, the lights danced over a large stone statue in the center of the circle. A shudder tracked through her as the illicit goings-on were high-lighted in glaring detail. She fought a gag as a plump naked octogenarian bobbled past her.

With a shake of her head, she whispered, "I'm blind."

"First, breaking and entering and now peeping tom. You get around, Xandie Meyers."

The voice was a soft, gravelly growl beside her ear.

"Lucky, I guess." She closed her eyes in disgust. Who else could have caught her in this weird situation if not Braun? *Well, you did ring him. Who else would you expect?* "Yay for small town policing. You caught the owner standing in her yard. Good for you. Could you remove the weird naked ladies?"

"Define weird naked ladies." Zach Braun smirked. "The police department always aims to please."

"Argh." Xandie waved her hand at the group of

naked ladies still dancing. "Deal with it, please."

Swallowing his humor, he cleared his throat. "Attention, nude dancers. You are on private property, please show yourself."

Xandie winced at his words. He was about to identify more than their names. The ladies lined up with hands on hips, facing the police chief and Xandie. At least he respected the naked dancers and kept his eyes at face level. Maybe self-preservation, though. The women were old enough to be his grandmothers. "Smart moves, policeman. You're sparing yourself years of therapy."

"Zachary is always a gentleman first and policeman second." A short and plump senior citizen bobbled and jiggled as she tittered.

"Besides," a purple-haired lady with a broomstick tattoo on her arm interrupted, "plenty of us have seen hairy Braun bottoms, including his mother's. God rest her follicle-challenged soul."

Had his mother died too? She felt a kinship with the annoyingly good-looking law enforcement officer. "I'm sorry. I didn't realize your mother had passed away."

Braun looked horrified, then sighed. "She hasn't. Mom stopped getting her waxing done at the hairdresser in town."

Broomstick tattoo leaned in close. "She is a hirsute woman. If you know what I mean." The woman waggled her eyebrows at Xandie who'd frozen, her back arched as if a stray breast had attacked her back. Shaking her head in confusion, she stepped forward with a save-me glance at the police chief.

"Ladies, I hope you got permission from Ms. Meyers about using her yard for your practice tonight."

Xandie shook head. "Nope, no permission. Otherwise I wouldn't be here tormenting my psyche."

A woman cleared her throat while the other five stared at her. "Well, I rang once, but no one answered. I assumed it'd be okay. Sera never had a problem with us sky clad in her backyard."

Xandie muttered, "My great-aunt needed glasses, otherwise she'd have died from the shock of too much old skin."

The law officer took a deep breath as if to control the snicker that kept escaping. He waggled a finger at the octogenarian. "You get permission. You know the town rules for your rituals, ladies. Don't make me arrest you."

In a coordinated move, they giggled and fluttered

their eyelashes. Xandie shuddered. What was scarier? The murder? Or six nude octogenarian's flirting?

"Ladies." Zach clapped his hands. "No more practicing, I'd hate for you all to burn out for tomorrow night."

Ogling his jean-covered bottom, they filed past to pick up their robes. All except one of the hairdressing crones with pink hair and purple highlights. She stomped up to Xandie and glared. "Sera wasn't a witch, but she had respect for our beliefs. She let us go through the library for our spells. She even joined in sometimes, but you aren't living up to her promise. You're neglecting your role as librarian. I'm betting requests have built up. It would disappoint her to see your lack of progress." She grabbed the last robe and stalked away, still naked, toward her car.

Xandie's eyes must have opened wide during the whole debacle since a damn bug flew into her right eye. Rubbing at the offended pupil, she glared at her nemesis. "You allowed them to get away with trespass and verbally attacking me?"

"Hey, don't blow up at me. Sera always allowed them to do whatever. Plus, I wasn't handcuffing them. They'd have me up on sexual harassment charges in the blink of an eye. Those women are vicious when thwarted."

Xandie blew her annoyance out with a breath. "Let me guess. You don't think I'm doing a great job as librarian either." She'd meant to sound sarcastic, not forlorn, but that's how it must have sounded, judging by Zach Braun's alarmed face.

"Don't fold on me." He placed a hand on her upper back and shepherded Xandie back inside the house and into the kitchen. There he sat her on a stool and got the fixings out for a hot chocolate, putting together a decent shot of liquid sugar.

Xandie made a surprise mewl, not unlike Theo, as she sipped it.

He shrugged. "Your great-aunt liked sweet drinks too. My mom and Sera were friends. I used to hang out here as a kid." He held up a hand to forestall any words from Xandie. "And no, you're not a bad librarian. Just find your own way. The library understands more than you realize. Just commit."

She snorted hot chocolate up her nose in shock. He knew about the library.

"Like I said, I spent time here. *And* I'm a shifter. Have an issue? Go to Ms. Sera and Theo will help you."

Shifter? Xandie placed her mug on the bench.

"You mean like a werewolf? Something bit you and now you change into a meat-seeking furry wolf?"

"Wolf?" Zach growled in disbelief. "I was born a shifter. Yes, I shift into a different species, but I am not a meat-seeking wolf. Spend time in the library. Ask it who I am." He cleaned the counter and dumped the dishrag into the sink. "If you wish to stay, rethink your human misconceptions." He paused. "Not everything is as it appears. You need to open your mind, or you'll stumble." With a quick pat to a smug Theo, he left.

"Consider yourself schooled, Alexandra Meyers." Come to think of it, why wasn't she more shocked? Okay, the naked dancing had thrown her. Then Braun's declaration of shifter status, she should laugh at him and call a mental hospital. So why hadn't she? Something inside her believed him, not shocked at his words...but why? Xandie left the kitchen but hesitated in front of the library door. She laid her palm flat on the heavy wood door. It pulsed warm, welcoming her. Zachery Braun had a point. She had to research, ask the library for advice and above all, be the librarian the library needed.

She needed to know what waited for her in Point Muse. Because if she stumbled, it might not hurt her.

It could kill her.

FIVE

"You did what?"

"It's the most practical solution for everyone."

"There's no everyone. There's just me. You had no right, Dad." Practical solution? This was *her* life.

"I'm your father. I have every right when you aren't thinking straight. Get rid of Sera's place and come back to Andrews and the College. Your job is waiting."

"Job? I'm shelving college kids' unwanted books while my dad stands behind me, making sure I do it correctly. Sera's house and the estate give me another way of living. One I'm enjoying." *Except for naked jiggling octogenarians. Those she could live without.* Her father's disdain of her choice rang crystal clear.

"Point Muse is not a way of life. It's a poison that will ruin your life, like hers—" His voice cut off.

"You mean mom?"

"Your mother disappeared in there. Sell the damn house. Get far away before it takes you down with it," he replied in short choppy sentences.

"Mom disappeared after we left Sera or are you referring to the fact mom's family comes from here?" Dead silence on the other end.

"Your mother didn't want that world."

"Why did she keep coming back? Why bring me to visit Sera after you said no?" Xandie still remembered her mom getting excited the closer they got to Sera that last visit.

"I. Don't. Know." Her calm unruffled father yelled the last few words.

"Mom still has family here. The lady at the bakery is a Harrow, same name as mom's before she married you."

"Sign the contract. I'll email it to you. It's a fair price."

Her father changed the subject again. Refused to talk any more about Point Muse and Xandie's mom. "Three months before I can sell, Dad. I told you I want to stay, find out more about mom's family."

"You'll receive nothing but regret. I'll send you

the contract. Otherwise that damn library will take over what's left of your life." With that, he hung up.

Xandie growled and threw her phone, narrowly missing Theo who gave her the evil eye. What a time for mobile reception to work. She could have done without that lecture. *"He decided to sell. He wants me back. Nothing about what I want."* Xandie sagged against the plump cushions of the couch. No matter what her father said, Sera left the house to her. "That's it, Theo. No matter what he says, I'm staying."

Theo jumped up and purred against her leg before he leaped off, heading for the library.

He was right. She had hours to fill in before the ceremony started. "Time to get serious, oh feline guide to the Great Library of Alexandria." Trailing Theo, Xandie headed to the library and opened the door. Where to start? She'd shelved the books away yesterday. So, what to do now?

Theo meowed and battered a pile of notes to the floor. "Geez, cat, I'm not your housekeeper."

Theo swiped at her arm with claws partially sheathed.

"Man, you are a temperamental feline." She shuffled the papers and read the top note. "Information on mating rituals of selkies?" *Wow, a zinger of a topic to start.* A muffled bump behind Xandie surprised her, and she spun. A gilt-edged book had fallen off the shelf and opened onto an involved diagram on selkie mating practices. "Holy flying books, Theo. The library is alive." Xandie grasped the book. "Okay, I have the selkie porn. What do I do with it?" Xandie's necklace heated for a second or two before cooling. A fire-engine-red appointment book lying on a large heavy wooden desk opened to a date three days from now. "Selkie good times gets a date with the library?" Xandie nabbed the pen and scribbled selkie rituals in the ten o'clock slot. The imprint glowed gold and a sweeping line of writing appeared. *Invitation sent.* Xandie shot Theo a surprised glance. "I write a name and the library invites the person or people involved to read the information here?"

Theo meowed an affirmative.

"What happens if access is denied?" Xandie up picked the next note and spoke aloud. "Information on migration patterns of battle ravens?" The date book flicked to another page. She scribbled in a blank spot and *invitation sent* appeared again. "Well, okay. Let's get to it." She settled in and powered through her pile until only two requests were left. An information request on the Leyden Papyrus, a text with ninety-eight spells in it and a personal notation from Professor Amoru. She waited, but it stayed open on the previous page. She quirked an eyebrow.

"Are you saying no to the spell and the professor, or just the professor?" A scroll slid out from a pile and partially unwound. She picked it up and tried to unroll the rest of the way, but the Papyrus refused to move. "So, they only get a portion of the spell scroll? How do they access that bit without visiting?"

The cat padded toward a set of connecting doors that a stack of shelves disguised.

She opened the doors and found a tiny windowless office that had a small desk, filing cabinet and a bright shiny photocopy machine. Placing the scroll on top of the glass she pressed the copy button. "I hope the library *is* a magical place. Because otherwise I'm sure this will destroy the scroll." The machine glowed, but no paper shot out. Xandie checked in case of a paper jam. But there wasn't any paper. She opened the paper draw. No paper, and no packet anywhere in the office. "Is stationery supplied?"

She lifted the scroll from the copier and walked to the appointment book. Still open, but on today's date. Gold writing glowed again: *information sent*. "I understand. The machine is magic and sends information out to the person who requested it." *Wow, saving on stationary costs.* She snickered to herself and dealt with the final request, Professor Amoru. She scribbled the professor's name on the open page. A zap of blue electricity arced from the page and Xandie dropped the pen, cursing. "The library zapped me."

Amoru's name glowed red, not gold. Text scrawled with slashing heavy black script: *invitation denied.* "The professor is persona non grata? Not allowed entrance?" Xandie's necklace tightened as if in agreement. *Okay, message received.*

Requests completed, she took a few minutes to tidy and shelve books, which had mysteriously appeared while she'd been occupied with requests. She shelved the last book into the witch section and let her hand drift over the different spines of the books. "Dad said I'd find no answers on my mother from you. Is that true?" A shelf shuddered and a small volume covered in blue fabric slid out. *Harrow family, Point Muse.* She ran a finger over the script. "My mom's maiden name." She scanned the contents page and found a family tree entry. Xandie rifled through until she found the page... And there was her mother's name in curling black script. *Miranda Harrow.*

Lila's name appeared too, a niece to her Mom. Xandie had family still alive and living. She rocked back on her heels, shocked.

"I was five when Miranda disappeared. I remember the old women wailing and crying."

Xandie jerked in response to the voice, the breath catching in her throat. She hadn't heard anyone come in. Lila stood at the entrance with two takeaway cups and an oil-stained bag in hand. "Thought you might crave sustenance before the ceremony tonight."

The air gusted from her mouth as the tension seeped from her. "Yeah, I could use a sugar hit."

"Hot chocolate with extra marshmallows, plus extra honey butter puffs."

She reached out. "Bring it on home to the hungry librarian."

Laughing, Lila handed over her goodies and perched on the corner of the desk. She leaned over and peered at the tome. "I don't remember Aunt Miranda much. She was my mom's older sister. It devastated Mom when the news of Miranda's disappearance hit. The family tried to find her, but no trace. Sera found zip, but the library kept whispering to her. She never worked out why. Mom said your great-aunt was so glad you'd survived your mother's fate she didn't fight when your dad took you away. She wanted you safe."

"Mom never spoke about Pont Muse. Not to mention, witches. Nothing. But I remember her bringing me here. She'd get excited when we'd come. Then revert to her normal calm self when we left. Which mother was real?"

Lila shrugged. "Both. Miranda showed no aptitude for earth witch powers. That's the Harrows, earth witches. One with nature and all that garbage. Well, at least some of us are." She grimaced. "I don't have earth gifts either, except a talent for inducing positive feelings in my baking. I'm betting Miranda was the same. No obvious talents. It's hard to live and deal with family when you lack any flashy witchy gifts to speak of. I understand her desire to leave. But I guess she still needed contact, a sense of connection, if she kept coming back."

"Maybe. I had no one else except dad, his aunt and mom. He's an only child and his parents died when he was young. Sera raised him. And he hated the town and everything to do with it, including her. Once mom disappeared, he wiped his hands clean of Point Muse. I'm excited about having more relatives, but nervous too."

"They'll love you. A librarian in the clan is big."

Xandie forced a smile. "If my dad gets his way, I'll be out at the end of my three months. He has a sale contract waiting."

"Have you told him no?"

"This morning. But he hates this place so much he can't understand why I'd ever stay."

"Duh, unanswered parental questions." Lila rolled her eyes.

"Not just that. In the library today. I can't explain it, but I'm supposed to be here. I'm home."

"Good for you. Sera always knew you were the next librarian. She'd rave about you to anyone who'd listen."

She frowned. "Why the big shock then when I arrived?"

"No one imagined you'd give up everything and move here."

"Working for my dad wasn't much of a career. But the way the mayor talked of Sera and this new development, it surprised everybody when I inherited."

"I think..." Lila ground to a halt, as if picking her words with care. "The development is big news, but most people hate it. Except for the most influential people in town. The same ones that already have power but crave more."

She bet they did. "You mean the mayor?"

"Funnily enough, I'd say no. Oh, he needed access and hounded Sera, but I'm not sure regarding the land. Your lawyer did though, same with the original estate agent."

Xandie decided to trust Lila. "I think someone killed Sera. And if the agent wanted this land? Maybe she was killed too."

Lila blew out a breath. "Thank God. I thought I was the only conspiracy nut here."

She snorted. "Well, can't say this is normal for me. But for what it's worth, I think both women were murdered."

"Agatha Christie, Angela Lansbury, Nancy Drew, eat your heart out." Lila rubbed her hands in glee, seized her coffee and drained it. "Right, where do we start?"

"We need Sera's and the agent's autopsy reports and a medical expert to explain them."

"I can help with both problems. Follow me."

Xandie followed Lila and waited for Theo to saunter out. He fixed his bright emerald eyes on her before nodding and departing for the kitchen. He'd given his blessing for her murder hunt. She smiled to herself and caught up with her cousin. If only Sera could see her. So different to the strait-laced acad-

emic librarian her father expected. Her great-aunt
would have crowed in delight. Whatever happened,
the library had shaken the real Xandie Meyers free,
and she was here to stay.

———

"Please, Aggie," Lila wheedled, pulling out the big
guns. "This is Sera's great-niece. My cousin, Xandie."
She shoved Xandie forward until she almost toppled
onto the older lady.

Aggie righted her with a quick burst of strength.
For an old girl, she had a strong grip.

The police dispatcher leaned on her elbows,
contemplating the two girls. "Only a half-hearted
attempt at emotional blackmail. I'm disappointed,
Lila Harrow. Didn't your grandmother teach you
better?"

"I know, Aggie, but Xandie has the anniversary
tonight, plus your son wants to arrest her. We're
time-crunched."

"Please, Mrs. Braun. Someone murdered Sera,
but I need the autopsy for her and the realtor to
prove it. If it's because of the library, I might be
next."

Agatha Braun pursed her lips and narrowed her

gaze, pinning Xandie to the spot. "Why is my son trying to arrest you?"

"Why do naked old women dance in my backyard?" She shrugged. "It could be he caught me breaking and entering Sera's house and peeping on naked women as they danced in my backyard. I guess it doesn't look good."

Aggie chortled and slapped the desk. "Or he likes you and wants to keep you around."

She choked on her spit. "I don't think so."

Lila broke in. "Aggie? What's the decision?"

Aggie opened a drawer and took out a couple of pages of printed paper.

"There. I copied it for you. Figured you'd be here, eventually. You better scoot if you don't want Zachy bear to rumble you."

Zachy bear? Xandie smirked. One for the humiliation file for use later for maximum impact.

Lila buzzed a kiss on Aggie's cheek.

Xandie nodded her thanks and let her cousin drag her out of the station and onto Main Street. *"Now what?"*

Lila towed Xandie into the bakery and waved to her employee as she sailed past into the back office. She slammed the door shut behind them. "Now we wait for my medical expert."

"Who is?"

"Your aunt, Amelia Harrow." A tall, skinny, auburn-haired woman flung open the door and stepped inside, slamming the portal shut behind her. She crossed the floor and snatched Xandie in a bone-crunching hug. She let her step back but kept a grip on her niece's hands. "You have your mother's stubborn chin and her eyes, but Sera's face shape."

Overwhelmed, Xandie nodded like a bobble head figure.

"One of the worst days of my life when Miranda left with you." She released Xandie but gave a pleased humph. "But we have you now and you're the librarian. The Harrow family is blessed to have you. And I'm delighted to have my niece back."

"Yeah, hi, Mom. Nice to see you too."

Lila's mother waved a hand in her direction. "Ignore my daughter. She's a drama llama. Miranda was my big sister. We were only a year apart." She smiled wistfully. "We fell pregnant at the same time and she even came back here to have you."

"She gave birth here?"

"Oh, Nickolas fought it, but she wouldn't budge. You girls were born a week or two apart. Lila first, then you came along. As soon as she could travel your dad ushered you away." She cleared her throat. "But now you're here."

"Hey, Mom, how about we leave the welcome speech for the moment? Time's getting away from us." Lila waved the autopsy reports in the air.

Amelia sat and wiggled fingers at her daughter. "Give it to me."

Lila handed them over before whispering to a still-speechless Xandie. "Mom's a vet, but she likes to read up on medical advances, autopsies, poisons, et cetera. For human and animal. She's weird, but the animals don't care. Plus, it helps she's a Harrow and can talk to them."

"She talks to animals?"

"My Harrow gift, darling. Now, shush, girls, let me work!"

Lila poked her tongue out at Xandie. Who giggled in return. Her cousin felt like an old friend.

After a while Lila gave up waiting and took refreshments from the bakery for the girls to gnaw.

Xandie had inhaled her third donut when her aunt sighed and sat back.

"Well, Mom? Did you find anything suspicious?"

"Sadly, yes. But remember I'm a vet, not a human doctor, but certain aspects of both autopsies are a concern."

Xandie choked her mouthful of donut down. "Worrying how?"

"I'll start with Louise Maker. We know the family and they're gray witches."

Lila explained to an ignorant Xandie. "Gray witches do middle-of-the-road stuff, not pure earth witch, but not dark magic. They're in between."

"Lack of commitment I call it. Can't be white or dark so have a little of each. Put up or shut up I say."

"Mother." Lila tried to divert her mom from a well-worn argument.

"Fine. Louise died late the night before last. After ten p.m."

"After I talked to her that night."

"Possibly. The wires were stripped from the coffee pot cord and the faucet has a leak. The coroner thinks she plugged the pot in with one hand and turned the metal faucet off with the other. Normally not an issue, but the landlord is remodeling, and the safety switch wasn't working."

"She fried?"

"Goodness, daughter of mine. There's no reason for crude comments. But yes. She hit her head but was dead before impact."

"An accident?" *Poor woman.* Whatever the woman's plans, she didn't deserve to die.

"On the face of it, yes, but I know she only brought that machine a few days ago. I was eyeing it off myself and she beat me to it. No way those wires and cords were stripped when she bought it."

"*Murder*. What else does it say, Mom?"

"Full rigor set in by the time police arrived. There was a purple-blue tint to the right side of the body, because of how she fell. Gash on temple and lack of blood show she was dead when it occurred. Burns on fingers of both hands. Consistent with death by electrocution. The landlord told her not to touch any switches as the building was being rewired that day. She ignored the warning."

"And the murderer guessed Maker would ignore the warnings," Lila muttered. "She was a massive caffeine addict. In here multiple times throughout the day getting double caffeine shots."

"Murder?"

Aunt Amelia nodded at Xandie's question. "That's what the coroner's concluded. Chief Braun will investigate this as a murder."

She groaned. Chief Braun hated her as it was. Xandie Meyers, suspect number one. Plus, she had a meeting scheduled with the victim that morning.

"And Sera?"

Thank God for Lila asking. Xandie didn't know if she wanted the death confirmed a murder.

"Sera was a friend, but I warned her not to be complacent. I told her to train you earlier rather than later. But she was stubborn. Thought she had years."

"Mom," Lila growled at her mother. "I'll cut you off from your mocha latte."

Amelia drew back, offended. "No need for nastiness, child of my loins."

She threw her hands in the air. "Yes, yes, we've established I'm a horrible daughter. Now get on with it."

"On the surface, Sera drowned while swimming."

"On the surface?" Xandie stared at the desk, unable to meet her aunt's gaze in case she turned into a blubbering mess.

"Typical findings in relation to accidental drowning and a cardiac arrest. Water found in lungs. Lungs over-inflated and heavy with fluid. Shows subject submerged in water at time of death. Full autopsy performed including toxicology screening and histologic analysis of organs, including lungs, kidney, et cetera. Small amount of alcohol found."

Lila smiled. "She liked the odd tipple. Her favorite drink was gin and bitter."

Amelia frowned at her daughter. "For the breakdown of cardiac muscle fiber, the coroner suspects cardiac arrest may have happened while swimming because of her age."

Xandie frowned. "I thought she drowned. And you mentioned everything looks normal. What makes you suspect murder?"

"First, if she had a cardiac arrest while swimming, she'd have lapsed into unconsciousness and drowned, anyway. Second, the chief requested a gas chromatography on Sera."

"And?" Lila prodded her mother.

"The only reason to do the chromatography is if he suspected another cause was at play. And he's right. She had aconitum alkaloids present. You can see it with a chromatography test."

"What does that mean?" Xandie couldn't stand the pressure any longer and paced.

"Aconite, or more commonly Wolfsbane, poisoned her. Levels were higher in her liver and kidneys."

"Wouldn't she have known she was poisoned, Mom?"

"Not necessarily. Her food or drink could've been dosed. Wolfsbane is bitter so something had to mask the taste. Witches use it in spells; Hecate herself created it. The root's soaked in a liquid and that becomes the poison."

Lila snapped her fingers. "On the day she died, they held the council session at the Mayweather Inn. A lunch meeting to discuss the development neighboring Sera's land."

"Poisoned at the Inn? How?" Xandie collapsed on the chair.

Amelia considered the report. "The taste of the drink would've masked the poison and copious amounts of alcohol were flowing. When she arrived home, Sera would've felt queasy. But she loved her afternoon swim, and nothing would have kept her from it. Around two hours after lunch, dizziness would have set in, followed by headaches, confusion, and then ventricular arrhythmia and paralysis of the heart. She'd have lost consciousness and drowned." She reached out a hand to her niece, squeezing tight. "I'm sorry, sweetie, but she was poisoned. Probably at the meeting."

"The same people who will be at the ceremony. At your house. Tonight." Lila nibbled on a lip, worried. "What do we do?"

"Well, it's obvious, darlings." Amelia stood and grasped her handbag. "You investigate. But don't worry. The Harrows will be there in force to support you. Right now, my anorexic Siamese needs me. Be good." She waved goodbye as she left.

"And that's what I have to live with daily." Lila flung herself onto the couch in a dramatic pose.

Stifling a chuckle at her new cousin's histrionics, Xandie mulled the mystery of Sera and Louisa's deaths over in her mind. "Someone murdered them. But why? Was it for the land or the library?"

"Yeah, and what's the tie between the two murders?" Lila tapped her chin. "Louise died at the office by supposed electrocution. Sera died swimming at a beach, but ingested poison at the council session. Where's the tie between the two women?"

"And who owns the building where the agent died? I was her first client of the day and she wanted to discuss something, but never got a chance."

Lila's eyes grew wide. "Mayor Cummings and his sister own the building and he attended the discussion. Maybe he's our guy?"

"Rose Mayweather at the Inn said the mayor stalked Sera. Is it possible he killed them both?"

"But why?"

"The land. He said the by-law was common knowledge, same with the property reverting to the town. But he told me himself no one knew about the will and me being named the heir."

"Makes sense. It's prime land because of the development."

"And he'll be here tonight."

"But so too will the Harrows be. God help him, because the rest of the family won't."

Sometimes it was nice to have family.

SIX

"Oh good gracious. Shoot me." Xandie rolled her eyes as another fully clothed octogenarian stalked past and threw her the evil eye.

"Wow, they're hating on you for kicking them off your property last night." Lila chortled and snagged free champagne.

"Please don't embarrass us, Lila dear. Remember the last time you drank champagne." Amelia grimaced at her daughter.

"Mom, I was twenty-one, and it was my birthday."

A Harrow cousin Xandie had just met chimed in. "Plus, we spiked the punch with morning glory." Lila and the new cousin, Holly, high-fived.

"I didn't hear an admission of previous misdoings, did I?" Chief Braun slid in close.

Both girls turned wide eyes on the law enforcement officer resplendent in a pressed black uniform. "Nope," they chorused.

Amelia let rip an elegant snort. "You were in as bad a condition as those two troublemakers, so I wouldn't mention past misdeeds."

Zach leveled a twinkling gaze on Xandie.

"Don't look at me for a confession." She winced when she realized what she'd said, and judging by the awkward silence, so did everybody else. "Nerves. Meeting everyone en masse is overwhelming."

Aunt Winifred, the youngest of her mom's sisters, patted Xandie on the back. "Harrows are scary by themselves. You add in the rest of town and it's a horror show. We understand."

Braun nodded to the Harrows and focused on Xandie. "Please try not to commit any more felonies tonight."

She fought the urge to poke her tongue out. "Why thanks, Zachy bear. I'll take that under advisement."

He sighed. "Let me guess. You went to my mother for the autopsy reports. She's the only one who calls me Zachy bear."

What to say without getting his mother in trouble? "What makes you say that?"

"My mom loves Lila like a daughter and she's thick as thieves with Amelia. She probably had the reports waiting."

"I refuse to either deny or confirm any wrongdoing which may or may not implicate me or anyone else." Ha, take her lawyer speak and shove it...

"Sorry to interrupt. Quick word?" Mr. Essam wiped his baldhead with a bright yellow handkerchief.

Poor man always looks nervous. She nodded and allowed him to tow her to a quiet spot. "How can I help you, Mr. Essam?"

"Well, it's about your estate."

"And?"

"You might be unaware, but a corporation has bought the lot next to your great-aunt's house."

Xandie held up a palm to stop him. "You're interested in my land."

He cleared his throat. "I have a client who is interested, and I have a contract ready. The price is generous."

"You and my father are preaching from the same hymnbook."

"Excuse me?"

"No, you're not excused. As my lawyer, you know I can't sell for three months."

"Everything's negotiable. And my client wants to set up their new resort right here. A money-making opportunity that will generate tourist dollars. Obviously, your land is in a better position than their second choice near the entrance to town."

She cut him off with a slice of her hand. "Over my body will this house sell."

"That's why I'm trying to help you. Before someone finds your dead body." Essam shook his fist, losing his mild, nervous demeanor in the face of opposition. "My family line comes from Egypt. The women in the family are all seers. The males get nothing...normally. But I receive feelings and dreams. And I've a feeling about you dying and this place is the cause. You need to sell it before it happens to you. You should be worried."

She shook her head. "If I were you, I'd worry more about what I'll do if you keep threatening me." She pushed past her lawyer and leaned against a statue. "Jerk."

Professor Amoru paused. "Is this a general commentary on the state of mankind or someone more specific?"

"Everyone wants this place and people are resorting to threats to get what they want."

"Ah, the nervous Mr. Essam, I presume." He lifted a white-tufted eyebrow in query.

"I die if I don't sell."

Amoru shrugged. "Humans die, that's the whole point of their life."

"Humans? Their? Surely that means you too?" A strange way to put it. Almost implying he wasn't human himself.

"Of course. Don't worry about the others. Stick to your purpose. Sera was stubborn to a fault, but she never wavered. I think you might have that in common with her."

"Strong will is a family trait, but from what I hear, quite a few people wanted her estate. Did you argue with her?" *How do you answer that, Professor?*

He nodded with a sad smile. "We argued nonstop. She refused me entrance, but never told me why."

"But you still kept asking, pushing?"

"I did. She was a fiery woman. We both enjoyed our encounters." He stared off into the waters of the bay. "I have done things in my long life for which others would condemn me. But arguing with Sera became the highlight of my stay. I didn't hurt her and wish no ill will upon her great-niece either. But I offer a piece of advice."

"Even if I say no, you'll still give the advice?"

Amoru let out a bark of laughter. "You are correct. But my advice is this. Keep your mind and your heart open. There are people who can help. Ask them." He bowed. "I need to pick my viewing spot. Can't miss the fireworks." The professor retreated and blended into the crowd.

A strange man. One she found equal parts creepy and interesting.

"Charming the locals with your sparkling wit? Or planning a heist?" Braun sauntered up with a smirk on his face at the disappearing professor.

"I'll have you know people love me." Xandie scowled at Chief Braun. "Isn't there a law about stalking me on my property?"

"I'm an invited guest."

"I have to talk to the invitation committee about their standards."

"Alexandra Meyers?" An older, skinny lady with hair scraped back into a bun stood nearby tapping her foot.

Xandie breathed a sigh of relief. Distraction was what she needed. "That's me. How can I help you?"

Xandie smiled triumphantly at Zachary *pain-in-the-neck* Braun.

He whispered in her ear. "Stay out of my investigation or I'll arrest you."

Whoever the human distraction, it was a sign from above to run. "Local law enforcement is sometimes a tad overbearing."

The older lady gripped Xandie by the elbow and dragged her over to the spot where the anniversary ceremony would take place. "There. Can you do anything?" The woman waved at a small pond in the center of the Grecian statue garden.

"About the statues?" She scratched her head, confused.

"Specifically, the surrounding plant life." The older woman huffed and ripped out a weed.

"To be honest, I'm not much of a gardener. They could be weeds or plants for all I know."

"They ruin the formal nature of the ceremony. They need removing."

"You mean the ceremony I only approved yesterday?" No way would she allow a demented stranger to give her orders. "Who are you again?"

The woman tilted her chin. "Irene Cummings. The mayor's personal assistant and the coordinator of this year's anniversary ceremony of the settlement of Point Muse."

"Oh, the mayor's sister." Now the officious woman made sense.

"I'm the coordinator of this event and the site is a disgrace. It was like Sera to let the gardens go to spite me."

"Sure, my great-aunt could've cared less about spiting you. Odds are these plants are just decoration."

"You refuse to remove them?" The woman glared poison daggers at Xandie.

"The ceremony's due to start soon. Maybe there are other things to occupy your time."

Irene grabbed two plants, trying to yank them out. She gave up and kicked them. "If anything goes wrong, it's on your head, Ms. Meyers." She gave her a similar evil eye to the ones the now-dressed octogenarians had cast at her and stomped off.

"Making friends with my sister?" Nigel Cummings stood close, wavering on his feet with a glass of champagne in hand.

She winced. Politicians made the worst drunks. She pasted on a fake smile. "Sorry. The plants upset her."

"Irene's intense. She's my older sister and always

looks after me. Been that way since before our father passed."

Not a mummy's boy, but a sister's boy. "I'm sorry about your father."

He shrugged. "It was a long time ago. He was barely home, and when he was, he focused on Irene. Daddy's little Princess, I guess." He toasted her. "I'm sure you're daddy's princess too."

And there was the awkward. "I upset her. I guess she wanted everything right for the ceremony today."

"Organization's Irene's thing. She'll calm afterward."

And the universe help her if she didn't.

"Ms. Meyers. Your attention, please."

Great. Grumpy Irene back for a second round. Xandie grimaced. The mayor winked and drained his wine, waving as he wandered away.

"Ms. Meyers?"

Irene's strident tones pricked at her self-control. Aiming for courteous, Xandie spun to face Irene.

"Ms. Cummings, anything else?"

"You refused to help with the weeds, but you're still the owner of this property," Irene muttered under her breath. "Such as it is."

"I'm sorry?" Xandie arched an imperious

eyebrow, copying her father's patented student intimidation look.

"We need more seating and extra lighting pointed at the assembly area. This would be beneficial for the ceremony." The mayor's sister stood with hands on hip, daring her to refuse.

Gritting her teeth, Xandie complied. "I'll see what I can do, Ms. Cummings."

She ignored Xandie and swung away, marshaling her troops.

And that was her dismissal. Xandie trudged toward the house. Sera had chairs stacked in the garage and there were extra switches near the library for more external lights.

She breathed a sigh of relief as she entered the house and gained peace and quiet. Plaintive yowls from the pantry had her crossing the floor in a hurry. She opened the door and Theo shot out spitting and hissing. "How did you get caught in there? I shut you in upstairs." Theo stared at her like she was an idiot. "A talking feline would be useful right now." She straightened. She might as well check on the library. Make sure no one had gotten in. Outside the welcoming room, she fell over a broken chair.

"What the heck?" She kneeled and clutched a chair leg. "How did this break?" Gripping the piece of timber, she eased the door open and felt for the light switch. "I locked this earlier, I'm sure." An electrical current fizzed, but the light remained off. "This is every horror movie I've ever seen." Taking a deep breath, she slipped inside. Shadows covered the bulk of the interior, but small puddles of light illuminated a disturbed room. Table knocked over, decorative vase smashed and phone in pieces. She tiptoed around the mess and tried the internal door.

"Still locked." She shifted, holding the wood leg outright. The place was bare, but if someone invisible attacked, she'd batter them to death with an antique. Xandie pushed the table out of her way and shrieked as she stumbled over something soft and lumpy. Propping herself up on her knees, she used the wooden leg to probe in front of her. She crawled forward but squealed when she placed a hand in a wet puddle. Her fingers drifted over a lumpy surface. Xandie flinched as she realized the lumpy surface was a human chest.

A loud buzz filled the air and lights blazed. She used her free hand to cover her eyes as she got used to the light.

"Oh, I don't believe it, she's killed him." A piercing shriek echoed around Xandie as she blinked like a myopic owl.

Irene pointed an accusing finger at Xandie. "Look at her, she's still covered in his blood and is holding a stake."

A throng of people blocked the doorway. She stared uncomprehending at her red-smeared skin. "Blood?" The soft, lump she'd bumped into had been a body. Her lawyer. The poor man who sported a matching chair leg to Xandie's twin. One that was currently sticking out from his eye.

"Oh, my..." She opened her fingers and her chair leg dropped to the floor. She scooted back from the corpse until she ended up against a pair of muscled legs.

A hand pressed on her shoulder.

"You need to come with me. You're under arrest, Alexandra Meyers, for suspicion of murder."

Chief Braun's neutral face swam into her view as he bent and hefted her up. "Murder?" she whispered. "He's dead?"

Braun shifted his gaze to the crowd of people hovering in the doorway as a man pushed through, accompanied by an attractive blue-haired woman. The man squatted down and immediately checked for a pulse. At the shake of his head, Braun turned again to Xandie. "Your lawyer is definitely dead, according to our esteemed local doctor and our best healer. Time to go to the station." He directed Xandie past the throng of interested observers.

Lila grabbed Xandie's arm. "I'll secure the house after everyone leaves and send mom to the station."

Amelia crowded in close, holding Theo. "Theo will be fine too. We'll sort this mess out."

She nodded blankly and tried to pat Theo, forgetting the handcuffs on her wrists.

"You messed this librarian thing up, didn't you?"

Her numb feeling wore off as the rough sarcastic words penetrated her brain fog. She looked for the speaker, but the voice matched none around her.

"I knew Sera was tripping on some homeopathic potion those Harrows pedal when she named you heir."

Xandie's eyes grew wider she focused on Theo. "Theo?"

"Right, only takes a corpse to hammer through your dense skull and get you to hear me."

Her. Cat. Was. Talking. To. Her.

"Welcome to the world of the Great Library of Alexandria, cupcake. Insanity is always the best defense," Theo hissed and flew out of Amelia's arms. Great, even her talking cat hated her guts.

Her day couldn't get any worse... *could it?*

SEVEN

"We're here to spring you from the pokey. You got those jailhouse blues yet?" Lila and Holly, Xandie's cousins, leaned against the cell as Aggie Braun let Xandie out.

"Now girls, be nice. She's had a trying time." Aggie patted Xandie on the back and gave her a quick hug.

"Ma, you baked cupcakes and bought her Lila's butter puffs and a hot chocolate twice a day. You also bought linen from our house and hooked up Netflix for her. Plus, it's only been a few days. She's not doing it tough." Zack Braun rested against the door-jamb of the cell area.

"Now, Zachy bear, you leave Xandie be. She's a sweet girl. We all know she's innocent of any crime.

No lip from you or no schnitzel tonight." Aggie whispered to Xandie, "He loves his mother's schnitzel, family recipe."

"Thanks for everything, Aggie. You're wonderful." Xandie gripped Aggie tighter. Without the police dispatcher's love and attention, the whole process of jail would have shattered her.

"Get out of here, girl, and attend the library. God knows what the backup of requests is like. Plus, it might be the library has answers for you."

"Thanks again, Aggie."

Lila and Holly grabbed Xandie and dragged her out to Aggie's desk. The girls peppered her with questions.

"Did they fingerprint you?" Holly jumped in with the first question.

Lila didn't give Xandie time to answer before she cut in. "Did they do a DNA swab, take your photo? Did they let you put make-up on first before your mug shot?"

"Okay, yes, they fingerprinted me and did a DNA swab. Braun interviewed me and they took so called forensic evidence and my clothing. Everyone was nice, and no one jumped me in jail. Can I go home now?" All Xandie wanted to do was take a bath, cuddle Theo and clean up the library backlog.

KELLY ETHAN

"Not yet." Braun placed paperwork and a bag on the table in front of Xandie. "Sign for your belongings and a list of your bail conditions. Plus, the date of your arraignment is in two days. You must be at the meeting, okay?" He gave Xandie a searching glance.

"I can't believe this. It's only been a couple of days and your investigation is already finished? From what Aggie has told me, the whole town thinks I did it. Do you?" For some reason, Braun's opinion of her mattered. Maybe she had a brain disease eating away at her logic centers. "You know I didn't do it, right?"

"He does." Zach's younger sister, Melody, clumped to a desk, sat herself down and sighed in relief as she popped a booted foot up. Following closely behind were Zach's Deputy twin brothers, Caleb and Riley.

Caleb nodded. "Yep, he has been a bear with a sore head since he arrested you."

His twin brother, Riley, agreed, "Yeah, he's a nightmare. Plus, Mom refused to do his washing if he didn't release you quick smart."

"Could you three shut up? Mom should have adopted you cubs out when you were born."

Caleb snorted. "Please, she couldn't get it right

98

with you, so she had the rest of us to make up for it."
He ducked when Zach threw a stapler.

"For Pete's sakes, you four. Let the girl go home."
Aggie slapped a hand on the desk.

"Fine. Keep your nose clean, Meyers. You need
to be squeaky clean for your arraignment, got it?"

"I got it. And since I'm not a murderer, it won't
be an issue." Xandie swept the bag of her belongings
up and sashayed to the door with Lila and Holly
trailing behind her. She exited the building and
breathed in the fresh air, lifting her face up to the
sun of the late morning. She closed her eyes a
moment and dragged in another deep breath.
Despite her release, a feeling of impending doom
hung over her. She still had to somehow prove to
Zach—and the townsfolk—that she wasn't a
murderer.

Before she could give any more thought as to
how she was going to do that, Lila linked arms with
her and gave her a tug to get her moving.

"Come on, Princess Jailbait. Let's get you back to
your royal crib."

Xandie gave a small grin and shook her head.

Sometimes Lila had a way with words.

Xandie waved to her cousins and closed the front door with a sigh of relief. She turned and peered through the window. A snicker escaped as she watched Lila and Holly argued over who would drive. Turns out, Holly was born only a month or two after Xandie and Lila. All three sisters had been pregnant at the same time. Gave Xandie a bond with her cousins she never thought she'd have. Still smiling at the squabbling cousins as they drove off, Xandie was about to turn away when she caught the flicker of a shadow out of the corner of her eye. Frowning, she squinted through the glass. It looked like a figure. Darting out from behind the house and down the driveway after her cousins.

Who would spy on her? The purple rinse naked set? Or someone a little more sinister? Or...maybe someone trying to break into the library. A sick feeling settled in the pit of her stomach then she pushed it away. No way was she about to give into the sense of fear that threatened to overwhelm her if she gave it headspace. Shaking off her suspicions and making sure she'd locked the front door, Xandie headed for the library. She wanted a jail-free shower but shuddered to think how much of a backlog waited for her in the library. When the police had finished with her house, they'd given Lila and Holly permission to enter and clean the library anteroom. Nothing scary should lurk in shadowy corners for her to discover now. Just the same, she opened the door with extreme caution, peering in to make sure.

The girls had cleaned the room, thrown away the broken furniture, and set the table back in its original spot. Best of all, nobody lay murdered on the floor. Xandie opened the internal library door in relief. Unchanged, the same warm, book-filled room.

Theo zoomed past, launching himself onto the desk and glaring at her.

Xandie smiled, almost glad to see him. She pushed the fact he'd talked out of her head. In fact, her time in the jail cell had convinced her she'd imagined it.

"I see they released you from the big house. Any jailhouse stories you want to share?"

Her mind hadn't played tricks on her. A talking cat wasn't her idea of fun. Theo sounded like a grouchy old man. "Nope, talking figment of my imagination. Nothing to report except the police imprisoned me for a crime I didn't commit." For some weird unknown reason, a mouthy feline seemed normal for her new life in Point Muse.

"Yes, I'm talking to you. And I'm sure most crims say they're innocent. Besides, you've got no upper body strength to slam a stake through the eye and into what was left of his brain."

"Left?"

"He was a lawyer. I rest my case." Theo coughed up a fur ball and shoved it off the desk and into the trash can.

Xandie heaved into her hand. "Okay, you are one filthy figment of my imagination. Nothing is worse than watching a cat vomit."

"Try being the one doing it." He patted a small pile of notes. "Only a few here. The library put a hold on requests until they released you. It likes you. Go figure."

Wow, rude much? She flicked through the requests. "Not too many here thankfully." She rolled her eyes when she found one from Professor Amoru. "Let's put that one to the side." The rest were routine. "Mating rituals for cockatrice and a basilisk, feeding patterns for carnivorous cryptids, housing regulations for Baba Yaga's giant chicken leg house. And legalities of a magically binding petition against the use of black magic within Point Muse surrounds. Normal day, hey, Theo?" Xandie pulled the appointment book out and scribbled inside.

"Do you classify normal as released from prison?"

Right, time to deal with one grudge-holding cat. "I didn't kill my lawyer, and I'm staying to help the library. What's your issue?"

Theo arched his spine, fur standing up. "My issue is Sera's dead and others are dying while you decide whether to play in Point Muse. Librarian, up and get to work. Find out who the killer is before they take you down."

"Wow, strong feelings for a cat. I get that you loved Sera, but I'm doing my best. I didn't grow up in Point Muse surrounded by all kinds of weird, plus a talking fuzz ball."

"Sera was a librarian. Protector and assistant to the Great Library of Alexandria, but she didn't own me. I've protected the library for centuries. I am the son of the last true librarian, Callistrius, and my full name is Theon. You'd do well to heed me." Theo bobbed his head, making sure she understood his words then licked his nether regions.

Yep, she respected his groin-licking wisdom all right. "You were human? How did you end up protecting the library as a cat?"

Theo stopped grooming himself and lowered his leg. "Bunch of stuff happened. A demon-possessed Caesar burned the library down and *bam*, I'm hand-picked to be a guardian."

"Why do I think you're telling little white lies?" The library's light pulsed brighter and Xandie arched an eyebrow.

Theo hissed at Xandie. "Fine, my father *was* the last librarian. He wanted me to be a scholar or a philosopher."

"And?"

"I wanted to drink more than study. I slipped a flask into the library and huddled in the rabid siren section looking at scrolls and Caesar."

Xandie snickered. "You were drunk, looking at ancient scroll porn. Classic."

"Excuse me? Do you want to hear this or not?" Theo glared before continuing, "A demon that wanted access to the library possessed Caesar. The library refused, and he retaliated with bale fire. My father was at the port picking up new scrolls and wasn't there at the time. Library protected her core and let its physical self, the actual building, burn, but she needed a librarian. I was the closest person. My physical self was gone, so she reconstituted me as a cat, a faithful guardian. She created the necklace as a conduit, Sera always wore the necklace. Although just before she died, she no longer needed to wear it to communicate with the library. The honor of serving as librarian passes through

Demetrius's lines. He created the library in the beginning, and it passed down to you, along with my guidance."

Man, the poor kid died and was now a nether-region-licking cat. Talk about an adjustment. Put her issues into perspective. "I'm sorry, Theo. I guess I need to figure things out and make sure the library's protected. Okay, Sherlock Holmes, here I come."

Theo dropped to the table and placed his paws over his face. "Try to stay alive and out of jail. That's all I ask. Oh, and listen to me sometimes."

"I've got this. Don't worry." She'd find Sera's killer and protect the library. Back to business, Xandie finished the requests and gave the library a tidy up. Hang on...the library knew everything that happened in the supernatural world. Xandie gripped the necklace around her throat. "Ah, library? Who killed Sera, the agent and my lawyer?"

A scroll flew out from the shelves and whacked Xandie in the chest. She grabbed the scroll and unrolled it. The library translated the ancient Latin into English before her eyes. "Knight's Sanguis. The Knights of Pure Blood." She frowned. "I shelved this earlier. When I asked about my mother and Sera and the library whispered blood over and over. But I didn't understand her." Xandie stared up at the light overhead. "You meant these guys, didn't you? Knights of Pure Blood?"

The light overhead pulsated furiously in agreement.

"Knights?" Theo spat. "More like killers."

Xandie scanned the rest of the scroll but it was a mishmash of first-hand accounts of survivors from Sanguis raids. "Why do you say killers, Theo?"

"They were Templar Knights. They'd bring in supernatural scrolls and books found in their travels. Sometimes they'd even protect the library from attacks. But as the world's human and supernatural populations grew, so did anti-super feelings within Templar ranks. A group split away; fanatics dedicated to pure human blood untainted by other bloodlines. They hunted down and killed anyone they thought supernatural. Many plain humans died, as well as those in the supernatural community."

"What did the Templars do?"

"They disavowed them, but the Sanguis still had high-placed Templars who supported them. Haven't heard from them for at least a hundred years though."

Xandie dropped into a chair and pushed her straight brown hair out of her face. The strands were all stringy since she hadn't washed it in jail. "You had to be a Templar to be a Sanguis Knight?"

"Once the Templars disavowed them, they recruited from family lines. Allowed the knights to marry and hide in plain sight in society. The training passed down from father to son. If they're active again, the deaths won't stop until they control the library or get rid of you. They're fanatics."

"So, guys with paramilitary training and Hitler delusions are alive and killing and in Point Muse?"

"Appears so. Watch your back and find them." Theo jumped down and sashayed to the door. "Time for a kitty litter trip. The tuna hasn't agreed with me." He shot Xandie an evil smirk and disappeared out the door.

Xandie shuddered at the thought of what tuna and kitty litter would do to her olfactory senses when she had to empty it. A scratching on the library window had Xandie shrieking. She dropped to the ground and peered around the desk and out the window.

A blonde teenager stood at the window with green nails extended, scratching on the glass.

Xandie open the window. "I have a door."

The teenager shrugged. Luminescent green and blue scales shot with silver appeared on her cheeks, then disappeared again. "I don't do doors. Mom says I'm a hazard when I'm inside." She flashed a toothy smile at Xandie and waggled her sharp, long green claws.

What kind of creature was she dealing with now? At least she knew the kid wasn't a fanatical knight out for her blood. "What can I do for you?"

The girl recited the message with a roll of her eyes. "While you were incarcerated, someone attempted entry into your house. We scared off one attempt and watched two other attempts thwarted by the library itself. We caution that the library must remain neutral in case it's used against all supernatural creatures. If you can't look after it, we demand the library appoint a more qualified assistant." The teenager took a gulp of air and studied her claws.

"Who are we?"

The girl snorted and a little trickle of smoke drifted away from her right gold-pierced nostril. She ran her tongue over pointed teeth. "The elders don't realize how pompous they sound. We used to eat humans. They sacrificed virgins to us. We will rule the world again. *Yada yada yada.*"

"Virgins?"

"It's a thing. Most of the younger gens have

moved on now. I mean how hard is it to find a virgin these days. You know?" She sneered at the thought.

Virgins, fried and eaten? "Dragon?"

She clicked fingers. "Give the librarian a prize, she got it."

"Your elders," Xandie stumbled over the word, "want me replaced?"

"Well, not all. Some are interested to see what you do. But the majority don't like you, or any changes in routine. They're giving you a week. Solve the murders and protect the library. Or they'll petition the library for a new assistant."

"That's a thing? They can remove me?"

"They can petition the library, so I'd get to it." The girl spun and headed down the path to the library's private beach. "Gotta go. The mermaids are laying bets on your survival. I don't want to miss good odds." She disappeared down the steps to the beach.

Xandie closed the window, still staring out through the glass. The library could remove her if she didn't find the killer and protect the library. She had no choice. She had to work this mess out. People trying to buy the library out from under her, bodies turning up, a murder charge and now a petition to remove her. "What's next?"

The library phone rang and Xandie stared at it like it was a striking snake or a bearer of bad tidings. She'd gotten used to limited phone coverage in Point Muse. Braving future misfortune, she answered, "Xandie Meyers speaking."

Irene Cummings steel-edged tones scratched down the line like fingernails on a blackboard.

"Ms. Meyers. This is the mayor's personal assistant. This is an obligatory notice to inform you of the Council's concerns over your behavior and your intentions toward the library."

"Intentions? I'm the librarian and I have no intentions except to do my job."

"Someone has placed a complaint against your great-aunt's estate, which lays out the terms of your potential disqualification. If proved, then the library and lands will revert to the council. Not your next of kin or the next appointed librarian."

"What?" The dragons wanted her out and now an anonymous complainer did too?

"You will have forty-eight hours to present your argument before an appointed panel decides the library's fate. I will inform you of time and place." With that, Irene Cummings hung up with a disdainful click.

Xandie had an arraignment for murder coming

up, and now she had to contend with a meeting to decide the library's fate? "Do you have any ideas about how to boost my luck? Because I think it sucks right now." Xandie's necklace tightened and warmed, but no other answers were forthcoming. "Is this a Sanguis Knight ploy, or a development land grab, or a group of supernaturals banding together to control the library?" Or was it the demon that had burned the library down centuries ago? "Too many suspects to choose from." Xandie stood and dusted her pants off. "Whoever it is, doesn't matter. I'm your assistant and that won't change." The game was on and she would win. Especially if she had her new family on board. Time for a visit to the sneakiest Harrow around...her cousin, Lila.

Xandie regretted leaving Sera's bike at home and hoofing it into town. What seemed like a quick bike ride now felt like a marathon. Thankfully, she'd left Theo behind, although he'd whined about her cruel captivity. He claimed he was worried about trouble but made a point of asking if she had a purse. Odds were, he was contemplating his stomach and Lila's bakery. Come to think of it, a butter puff wouldn't go astray. Xandie salivated at the image of the melt in your mouth pastry. So much so, she hadn't noticed the dark green SUV closing in on her as she walked along the side of the road.

The noise of the engine revving behind her drew her from the sugar-inspired fantasy. Xandie shifted farther over to the side of the road and waved the SUV past, but it continued to pace behind her, gunning its engine every so often. She slowed almost to a stop, but the driver did the same. Start moving again and so did he. Okay, this was definitely about her. It had nothing to do with whether she was taking up too much of the road. She had a stalker. A slow-speed vehicular stalker.

Sweat broke out on her forehead and she swallowed hard. Despite her silent admonition to not give into panic, her hand trembled a fraction as she grabbed her phone from her pocket and hovered a finger over the now pre-programmed Chief Braun's phone number. Although, who knows if she'd get through to him in time if there were trouble.

She glanced up and down the road. Halfway to town, but everything seemed deserted. The only human or supernatural resident building near Sera's place was Mayweather Inn—home of the lovesick Rose Mayweather. She hated to call Braun, but

Xandie was on her best behavior since released on bail. The last thing she needed was another encounter with Zachy 'bear' Braun. She'd deal with whatever happened. The SUV could just be a case of run-of-the-mill road rage. Xandie wiped sweaty palms on her jeans, tucked her phone away, and took up a jogging pace. Mayweather Inn wasn't too far down the road, if she could make it safe and sound.

The SUV sped up, coming closer and closer. Xandie's heart rate accelerated, the beat so loud she swore she could hear it in her head. Stomach muscles tightened. Her hands shook and so too did the muscles in her legs. For a moment she felt as if she'd pass out. Then she forced her sluggish brain to react. She quit looking over her shoulder and bolted.

The breath gusted from her throat. Her chest hurt as she dragged fresh air into her lungs and quickened her pace. The Inn's driveway lay up ahead. She was already running past fences that bordered the land. She willed her legs to move faster. *I can do this.*

Speeding up, the SUV narrowly missed Xandie. Hot air rushed past her, dragging sharp stones and gravel with it. She wrenched an arm over her face, wincing when rocks sliced tiny razor cuts over her protective arm. She snatched a large rock from the air as it headed for her face.

The driver slammed on the brakes and shot the car into reverse. Aimed straight at Xandie. She flung herself to the side, grazing jean-clad knees against the road. She toppled into a small ditch but forced herself upright then shot straight for the fences bordering the Inn.

"Have. To. Get. Over. The. Fence," she huffed as she reached the boundary line and hoisted herself up. The Inn, a public place, would stop anything else from happening. She turned and squinted at the car. If she could just see the license plate... "No...dice," she managed to get out, still perched atop the wooden fence and struggling for breath.

Mud covered the license plate, and the windows were tinted too dark for her to see if the driver was male or female. Still holding her rock, Xandie pegged it at the car and shattered a brake light at the back of the vehicle.

A whirlwind of dust and stones spun into existence as the murderous car took off. Xandie sagged on top of the fence before slipping down the other side and limping across the lawn to the stairs of the Inn.

"Honey, what have you done yourself?" Rose

opened the Inn's front door and stared at Xandie's disheveled state. "Didn't you get released today?"

Xandie hobbled up the steps and dragged herself inside with the help of a frowning Rose. "I swear I killed no one, and someone just tried to run me down."

"That's what you say." Aaron, Rose Mayweather's part-time love, glared at Xandie.

"Do you think I'd ruin brand new jeans just to pretend I'm a victim?" Xandie shot a near nuclear-strength glare back and pointed at the rips on her jeans and skin. "Shops in Point Muse aren't the height of fashion. Why would I risk my favorite pair of jeans?"

"Who knows what librarians think. None of you can be trusted with so much power."

Great, another suspect to add to the list. She sneered at Aaron but dropped it when Rose bent down and poked at her right knee. "Ouch," Xandie hissed and limped to the nearest chair.

"Aaron, stop your bellyaching and grab the first aid kit."

Muttering under his breath, he stalked off, returning with a lime green container.

Rose thanked Aaron and crouched next to Xandie. She peeled the torn fabric from Xandie's knees. "Trust me, sweetie. She didn't do this on purpose. No single woman wants scars." She winked at Xandie then was all business. "Come into my office so I can inspect your knees. Aaron, call Chief Braun and explain what happened."

"Why do I get the cop?"

"Because I'm the murder suspect and victim?"

Rose cleared her throat. "Unless you want to undress the poor little mite and doctor her cuts, it's the police for you." She waited until he disappeared and whispered to Xandie, "Aaron can't stand blood, but hates looking like a wimp even more. This way he still feels like he's helping."

"Didn't think he was the helping type myself."

Grabbing a pair of dressmaking scissors, Rose cut the legs off Xandie's jeans, leaving her with a pair of ragged shorts and pale legs. "He might surprise you. Aaron used to be in the Marine Corps, one of Aries descendants. But all the horror he saw gave him a blood phobia. Now he runs a local mechanics and bar tends here."

"Aries?"

"Greek God of war." Rose beamed. "I'm descended from Aphrodite, same pantheon of gods."

"Everyone says this stuff so matter fact. I thought I'd freak out more than I am." Xandie bit her lip when Rose dabbed disinfectant over her knees. All the supernatural goings on should have her knocked out on the floor. Déjà vu slammed like a freight train into Xandie. This whole freaky situation had that familiar feel of a well-worn sweater. Something worn often, but sometimes forgotten.

"Point Muse has always been a haven for the strange and freaky. Families from all different pantheons of worship, shifters, magical creatures and the occult have settled here." Rose slapped a plaster on the first knee and moved to the second.

"I'm not against the weird. I have a talking cat and a magical library."

Rose doctored the other knee and then disinfected her hands. "Someone means business if these injuries are anything to go by."

"You don't believe I killed my lawyer?"

"Honey, everyone's dreamed of doing that. But I think with those little arms, you'd have to have been very furious. And you don't strike me as a hold-a-grudge and kill-em-dead type."

"Thanks. I think." Xandie stretched her legs, wincing as the skin pulled. For all that Rose had a gossipy housewife vibe, she'd been efficient and calm about patching Xandie up.

"I've done this a few hundred times over the

years and I'm descended from the goddess of love. Trust me, I've had to patch up a few lovelorn boys in my time."

Had she read her mind?

Rose stood and patted Xandie on top of her head. "And before you ask, no, I can't read minds, but the subject comes up often." She paused for a moment. "Did you recognize them? The people who ran you over?"

"No, tinted windows. But I knocked a light out if that's important."

Rose nodded. "It might be. Aaron's garage is the only one in town, but he won't talk to cops. A misspent youth. Cops aren't his favorite people."

"Mine either," Xandie muttered under her breath. Aaron would speak to Rose, but Xandie didn't want the gossipy woman knowing her business. She could appeal to his better nature, his compassion, or maybe he'd take cash.

The door to the office shot open, giving a resounding bang as it thumped against the wall. Xandie jumped and twisted around in the chair to face the entrance, although she didn't need any second guesses to work out who it was.

"Here we go again, Meyers," Zach Braun growled as he strode in. He paused, hands planted on his hips as he stared at Xandie. The he sighed, moved closer and kneeled in front of her to inspect her doctored knees.

She scowled at him. "Except once again, I did nothing. I'm the victim."

Standing, he grabbed his phone out and typed notes. "What kind of car, who was driving and what happened?"

The three W's of crime. "A dark green SUV, tinted windows so I couldn't see who drove it and it forced me off the road. Reversed and tried to hit me again. I picked up a rock and pegged it at the back light."

"No idea who or what they were after?"

"Nope, except it's obvious I was the who. As to why, maybe they wanted to see me bleed?"

Braun stopped typing and shoved his phone away. "You are a serious crime magnet. I only released you this morning."

"Once again, not my fault." Xandie grimaced.

"Right. If you're satisfied with Rose's temporary doctoring, I can take you home or to the hospital."

Shuddering, Xandie shook her head. "Nope, people die in those places. Home is fine."

"Let's go." He nodded to Rose. "Thanks for the help."

"No worries, Chief." Rose wandered over to Aaron who stood outside the office staring at them. She whispered to him for a moment, before pasting a smile back on her face and waving as they left.

Braun helped Xandie hobble to a shiny police car.

"Let me guess. No way to tell who tried to hit me because too many residents in town hate me?" She eased into the vehicle and rested against the leather seat in relief. At least he hadn't hauled her off in handcuffs like last time.

Slamming the car door behind her, he jumped in the driver's seat and gripped the steering wheel. "Too much to ask you to stay safe and out of trouble?" Without waiting for an answer, he kicked over the engine, eased the car onto the road and headed back toward Xandie's house.

Xandie stared out the window at the scenery. She didn't think staying safe and out of trouble wasn't what Point Muse had planned.

EIGHT

"Remind me again why the three of us are skulking behind the town's garage when we should be waiting outside the council rooms?" Holly whispered to Xandie and Lila.

Lila rolled her eyes at her Harrow cousin. "Come on, Holly. Be brave. Take a chance. Aaron refused to speak to Zachary's brothers. Xandie has more of a chance if we try. And it's been two days since her gravel slide; maybe someone dropped the car off by now. We can get gossip on who her hit-and-run driver is."

"Would you two shut up?" Xandie hissed at her cousins. Sometimes family was great and sometimes they wouldn't shut up. "Does Aaron like either of you? Talk to you?" Surely, they had a one out of three chance he might tolerate at least one of them.

Lila grimaced. "He doesn't like Harrows too much. He's descended from Aries, strife, conflict and war stuff. Harrows are home and hearth, earth witch people. Except for our grandmother Elspeth, she's kind of a hag."

Holly coughed. "Speak for yourself. Ain't no earth witch here, unless you count buried in the earth."

Xandie rolled her eyes. "I'll never understand anything you Harrows say, will I?"

"She gets feelings, images, about people about to croak," Lila explained. "Too dark for the Harrows. Except for Elspeth, she's always dark. But Holly gets it from the sperm donor."

"Oh. My. God. Can you stop calling my father that?"

"Well, you haven't seen him in ten years, have you?"

"True," Holly spat out the word and grimaced. "Fine, you're right. But you need to understand he's Bansidhe. He has a family clan to care for in Europe. He couldn't stay here. Besides, I talk to him almost every night."

"Aren't banshees females?" Xandie fought her

inner hyena. Here she was talking about a mythical creature that proclaimed future death like it was a normal day. *For Point Muse it was.*

"Female dominant, but not female solely. Dad was an elder and floated around the world for a while before he found Mom and Point Muse, and then I came along. Ten years later, the call to bond to a family was too loud to ignore, and he had to go." Holly shrugged. "I guess you get used to not seeing a parent after a while."

"Harrow women raise Harrow babies. The men always seem to leave us." Lila wiped off imaginary dirt from her linen pants.

"Lila, your dad didn't have a choice. Hades needed him." Holly punched Lila on the shoulder. "Lila's dad, Harry, is Hades' underworld enforcer, has been for decades. He visits with her mom and Lila when he can."

"Great. We all have daddy issues. Can we please get on with grilling Aaron for details on my stalker car? I don't want to keep looking over my shoulder for Xandie-seeking car missiles."

Lila pointed at Holly. "I vote for the death chick. The stench of death has to be more appealing to an Aries descendent than a sweet baker."

Xandie pulled Holly up. "I'll try to get the info

out of him first. If he won't budge, I'll give you the signal like we planned, and you go in for the kill. Got it?"

"I still don't see why I have to do it," Holly grumbled but raised her hands in surrender when both girls glared. "Fine. You guys are so touchy."

Xandie concentrated on the peeling gray door of Aaron's garage. He wasn't the most welcoming of guys. She was a tad worried on how the plan would pan out.

"Courage, Cuz." Lila pushed the door open and dragged Xandie into the black pit of grease, commonly known as Aaron's garage.

"What do you want?" Aaron stood by his office door with his arms crossed over his massively built chest.

Rose must like them built like a tank. Wide shoulders, thick tree-trunk arms and his buzz-cut hair added up to a no-nonsense guy. Lila stayed in the doorway but shoved Xandie to the wolves, a.k.a. hulking Aaron.

"Hi Aaron, isn't it? You met me at Mayweather Inn." She plastered on the largest non-threatening smile she had.

He stepped back a few steps, blinking rapidly.

Okay, maybe not so non-threatening. She dialed

the wattage down. "Xandie Meyers. Rose cleaned my knees up after the accident." *Not so much of an accident.*

He nodded and pasted to scowl back on. "Yeah, she made me talk to the cops." "Sorry. I don't like law enforcement much either. Especially that pushy Chief Braun."

"What do you want?"

"How about we go into your office and have a chat?"

He shrugged. "Suppose it won't hurt me. Even with your murder rep I could take you. Come on." He inclined his head and invited her in.

Xandie gulped and slid into the office but stayed in view of Lila.

"Again, what do you want?"

"Has Braun been here asking questions about my run-in with the car? "

"Tried to talk to me, but I'm busy."

Straight to the point. "Have any green SUV's with black tinted windows and a broken taillight come in here?"

Aaron's face settled into a stone pattern. "I'll tell you what I told Braun. I'm a paper guy, no comput-ers. I'm still going through receipts. I'll let you know. Now get out, unless you have a car for me to fix."

Xandie held her hands up. "Whoa there. I don't want to upset you. I just need a little help is all." She coughed and wrinkled her nose at Lila. Getting the sign, Lila disappeared for a moment before returning with a bent-over and groaning Holly.

"Helping you will get me killed or bankrupt. Leave me and Rose alone, got it?"

"Look..." Xandie trailed off as Lila charged through the doors with Holly.

"Hey, we need help. Holly cut a hand on your door. She's bleeding." Lila waved Holly's red-covered hand around Aaron's face.

A face that turned chalk white and quivered like a bowlful of cottage cheese.

"I got a kit out back. I'll grab it, you doctor her then leave, got it?" He bolted for the door, yelling over her shoulder as he went, "and no suing. You aren't paying customers. It doesn't count."

Here's hoping the glove of blood coating Holly's hand was fake or Xandie was joining Aaron in the club of wimpy blood haters.

"It's sauce." Holly licked one of her fingers.

Xandie and Lila shuddered as one.

"Who's the coward now? Come on, or he'll be back in and my special effects will be pointless." Holly waved her ketchup special at her cousins.

"Fine." Xandie caught herself before she asked Holly if she wanted fries with that. She pawed through the mess on Aaron's desk. "Geez. This guys a pig. We'll never find anything."

"Germs are the only things we'll get from him." Lila screwed her nose up as a piece of lettuce stuck to her fingers. She shook it off, and it flew up and stuck to Holly's ketchup-covered hand. Lila snickered. "All we need is bacon."

Xandie tuned out her cousin's crazy antics and kept flipping through the paperwork.

"He said he's working on receipts now. Has to be on his desk somewhere." She moved his keyboard and flattened underneath was a receipt for a broken taillight. "Bingo." She waved the receipt at her cousins and stuffed it in her bra when she heard Aaron stomping back.

"Quick. Cover the hand up with this." Lila shoved an oil-stained shirt at Holly. "We don't want him to realize its sauce."

Holly grabbed the shirt, wound it around her hand and held it tight to her chest.

Xandie moved closer to Holly and Lila, pretending to inspect the injury.

"Here, doctor her up and get out. Shut the door when you're done. I'll be working out back." He

KELLY ETHAN

threw the kit at Lila and bolted again.

Holly whimpered as Lila took the bandages out and covered Holly's fake injury.

"Your injuries are fake. Why moan?" Xandie whispered.

Holly whispered back, "I have to make a sound in case he's listening. Plus, I've got cramps and a fierce craving for fries."

Lila whacked Holly on the back of the head. "Let's get out of here before he rumbles us, and we all spend the night in jail with a Chief tight-butt."

The girls nodded their thanks to Aaron as they shuffled a moaning Holly outside. They took their time, strolling down the street until they hit Lila's bakery.

Lila ushered them straight through to the office and stuck her fingers out for the receipt.

Xandie fished a hand into her bra, looking for the paperwork she'd stolen from Aaron's garage.

Holly covered eyes with her sauce-covered digits. "I'm too young to watch such antics. My innocence is in danger of corruption."

Lila snorted. "Please, senior year corrupted your innocence. Don't you remember the mascot fiasco?"

"I told you I had nothing to do with how that video got on the Internet. You were in charge of the ferrets, not me. That's all I've got to say." Holly jammed her hands on her hips, forgetting the ketchup, which speckled the area in a bizarre crime scene painting.

"Chupacabra. They were chupacabra you ordered, not ferrets. They ended up chasing the whole class. Everyone had to donate blood and you know how I hate needles."

"Guys?" Xandie waved the receipt in the air, but both cousins ignored her in favor of squabbling.

"Except you." Lila dramatically pointed at Holly. "You disappeared when it was blood donation time."

Holly cleared her throat. "About that."

Lila covered her eyes and slumped on the couch. "I don't think I want to know."

"When everyone was giving blood, I was under the bleachers with Caleb Braun, Zach's younger brother." Holly cringed waiting for the explosion.

"What?" Lila drew the word out, with the implied promise of future violence.

"He wanted to show me his roar under the bleachers."

Xandie snorted, caught up in the cousin's spat.

"What did I tell you about the Braun twins? They can't keep their fur zipped up."

"I swear it wasn't like that," Holly protested.

"It never is, sweetie. It never is." Lila shook her head in disgust.

Xandie intervened before the ketchup morphed into the real red stuff. "Anyone care to read the receipt with me or continue squabbling about your past flirts?"

Holly burst out laughing together. "He really was practicing his roar with me that day, Xandie. The Brauns are bear shifters."

"Oh. My. Goodness." That explained everything. Xandie slapped a hand against her forehead. "Braun is German for brown and his family comes from the Black Forest. Makes complete sense now."

"I guess unless you grow up here, it's hard to imagine people as a different species."

Xandie agreed with Lila. She'd have to process 'Zachy bear' another time. Now she had to focus on the receipt and who wanted to hurt her. She flapped the paper in the air again, this time grabbing everyone's attention.

Holly grabbed the receipt from Xandie's hand and read it aloud. "One tailgate light, green paint match. SUV Council lease."

Someone who worked for Point Muse council tried to run her down. "So, it's about the land, not my library?"

"Even if the council leases the SUV, it still means multiple suspects with motives." Lila paced through her office. "But the mayor has a council vehicle. Irene holds the purse strings, and she's cheap enough to lease rather than buy."

"The mayor had run-ins with Sera, according to Rose. Plus, he knew all about the development. He owned the building where the agent died, and he was at the anniversary ceremony when my lawyer died." She shook her head. "He's the mayor. Why would he want to kill people? He's in charge of the town anyway, so what's his motive?"

Snorting, Lila poked her head out of the office to check on the bakery before popping back in. "It's always about greed. Whether it's money or knowledge. Who knows? He's a politician, it's second nature."

"What do we do?" Holly curled up on the couch, nibbling on a nail.

Lila grabbed the receipt and held it out to Xandie. "Keep the evidence in your underwear. Safest place for it. As for our next move, we get Xandie to her council hearing and make sure she doesn't lose the library."

In the rush of investigating, Xandie had forgotten all about Irene Cummings, the council meeting, and about losing the library for good. No wonder her screwed-up priorities annoyed the cat.

Somedays she annoyed herself.

"Now, I want to remind people. This is a friendly meeting, just to air any issues and make sure Alexandra Meyers meets all requirements in accepting her inheritance and position with the library." Mayor Cummings smiled widely at the room of assembled do-gooders. "Let's get going. I'll open the meeting to the floor. Please state any grievances against Sera Meyers' beneficiary, and to the estate and the separate supernatural holding of the Great Library of Alexandria."

Gulp. "Sounds serious when he puts it like," Xandie whispered to her Aunt Winifred. Winifred had taken a year of a law degree at the community college next town over. This was the closest the town had to a lawyer now Neville Essam had died.

"Hush, dear. Look like you're taking this stupid farce seriously." Winifred sat bolt upright, blinking furiously.

Xandie guessed this was her aunt's version of serious.

One of the naked brigade waved her hand. "We have a complaint. She spied on us during our practice and made Chief Braun remove us from the property."

"I can answer to that complaint."

Zach Braun's growly voice was a welcome sound to Xandie's already-burning ears.

"The ladies taking part in the ceremony did not reach acceptable contact with the owner of the land. They did not ask permission. They also failed to inform the owner of their clothing optional state. The owner was within her rights to ask them to leave. The practice ceremony also started late night/early morning, interrupting the owner's sleep patterns and causing reasonable distress and disturbance." Zach sat and crossed his arms, scowling at everyone.

Aggie reached around her son and gave Xandie a thumbs up.

The mayor nodded his head gravely. "First complaint noted, defended affirmatively. The Council will disregard this point." He glanced at Irene and she stepped forward, reading a statement from another complainant.

"This is a general complaint on the character and suitability of the beneficiary of Sera Meyers' estate, one Alexandria Meyers." Irene paused for a moment before continuing, "It has come to the knowledge of the upstanding citizens of Point Muse..."

At this, equal amounts of laughter and agreement deafened the room.

Xandie peeked around. Most people were snickering over the upstanding citizen comment, but the older women were frowning and nodding. Not all of them were the naked octogenarians either.

Eyeing the culprits down, Irene continued, "Alexandra Meyers recently became the focus of a murder investigation and even arrested for it. This undermines the trustworthy characteristics needed to helm the library. The complainants request her removal, and the property reversion to council holdings. End of statement." Irene peered over the paper at the crowd. "Rebuttal?"

Winifred held her hand up. "Although my client has been a central suspect of the murder of Neville Essam, no proof is provided of any crime. This complaint is pointless until or if my client is proven guilty of this crime." She lowered her hand and smiled beatifically at the crowd of naysayers on the other side of the room.

"Way to go, Aunt Winifred". Xandie permitted a small glimmer of hope to grow. Only one year, but it sounded like she'd missed her calling as a lawyer instead of making herbal remedies and candles.

Braun stood again, this time with a sigh and a quick look over his shoulder at the door behind them.

Xandie followed his gaze, but no one was there. Who was he watching for?

"Six days ago, Neville Essam was murdered in the library's welcoming room. General statements of witnesses determine that Alexandra Meyers was found leaning over the victim, covered in blood, holding a chair leg. We found another chair leg to be the murder weapon. Also, the suspect was seen arguing with the victim, not long before the murder occurred. Subsequently, police arrested, but soon released her on bail while enquires are ongoing. Further investigation noted two other murders, that of Sera Meyers and Louise Maker, that share similarity. We concluded the suspect had motive for all three deaths."

He paused when Aggie tugged on his sleeve and showed him a text. "Can you excuse me for a moment, Mr. Mayor? Something has come up." Without waiting for acknowledgement, he strode to the door, opening it wide. Chief Braun's deputy and sister rushed to the door and handed him a file. After perusing the file, he slapped it against his leg as he strode back to the mayor.

"Apologies, Mr. Mayor. Forensic testing has come back. The test revealed the skin under the victim's nails does not match Alexandra Meyers' DNA. And none of the prints recovered from the murder weapon were hers. Her alibi for the murder of Sera Meyers and Louise Maker has also checked out. She wasn't in town for her great-aunt's murder and records show she received takeout at the approximate time of Ms. Maker's murder. Therefore, the police department of Point Muse drops all charges against Alexandra Meyers." He sat in a controlled manner, ignoring the furor that broke out around him. Aggie high-fived her daughter who'd scooted in next to her after delivering the evidence to the chief.

Xandie stared openmouthed at Zach. He'd cleared her. She wasn't a murder suspect anymore.

Winifred enveloped Xandie in a pillowy soft hug. "See, everything comes out the way it's supposed to be. Trust in the universe."

Irene cleared her throat. A frustrated expression crossed her face for a split second before clearing to her normal neutrality.

Xandie could have sworn the mayor's sister

wasn't happy about the decision to clear Xandie of murder.

"Great news, Xandie." The mayor beamed a fake politician smile out to the crowd, milking his spotlight for all he was worth.

But for all his pleasure at her non-murderer status, she noticed his knuckles were white. White from gripping the wood of his desk. Was it stress or anger at his thwarted plans? Xandie cocked her head to the side, examining Irene. All she showed now was disgust at the surrounding chaos. No, Irene Cummings was too uptight about law and order to stray. But would she cover up her brother's actions?

"Wait, wait. I have a complaint." A chubby man with bright gold hair and heavy rings on his fingers huffed and puffed up to the mayor and slammed a document in front of him.

Mayor Cummings calmed the crowd down with a hand wave as he read the papers. "Unfortunately, this seems to be a valid contract of the sale for the estate of the late Sera Meyers, in its entirety, to the consortium of Louise maker, Neville Essam, and George Mitas for one million dollars. Witnessed by a Nicholas Meyers. This breaks the conditions of the inheritance as set out by Sera Meyers herself."

This time the din of the crowd drowned everything except for the roar of blood in Xandie's ears.

Winifred shot her niece a worried look. "If you have something to tell me, now would be a great time."

Xandie shook her head, stupefied. Her father had signed the contract as a witness. She'd told him she wasn't selling. She thought when he'd stopped calling, he'd given in. Instead, he went scheming behind her back. She spoke in a normal voice back to Winifred. "I did not sign a contract. I never agreed to a sale. In fact, I told my father, Nicholas Meyers, I was not selling." She had no secrets to hide so why should she whisper. The town would find out soon enough.

"Indeed." The mayor confirmed Xandie's words. "Alexandra Meyers has not signed the contract."

Mr. Mitas swiped his palms down his dress pants. "Nicholas Meyers managed the sale on behalf of his daughter, Alexandra. He told us she was in complete agreement. In fact, he's here to testify." He pointed wildly down the aisle as Xandie's father slipped out from chair at the back of the room and marched down the aisle.

How had she missed him in the crowd? With her

father's disdain of Point Muse, he should stand out like a flare.

He refused to look at Xandie as he shuffled past. He moved up next to Mr. Mitas and the mayor. Nicholas frowned gravely out at the crowd. "I knew my aunt's property would be too much for my fragile daughter. She lost her job at a public library and was emotionally vulnerable. I contacted the estate lawyer and explained my concerns. He spoke to his associates, Ms. Maker, and their banker, Mr. Mitas. The offer was tended to me as my daughter's care-taker. Her signature was a mere formality. She would've agreed eventually."

Winifred sprung to her feet. "You stated she would've agreed, *eventually*. This implies she wasn't in agreement when the contract was drawn."

"Well, I mean..." Xandie's father seemed flustered for a moment before composing himself. "No, she hadn't agreed. But she will."

"That wasn't my question, Nicholas." Winifred shook a finger at Xandie's father. "I'm curious, was there a finder's fee by any chance?"

"A small amount. Nothing outrageous." He smiled coolly at Xandie, meeting her betrayed gaze. "You've no clue what this town is like. It sucks you dry until your nothing but a husk. I'm protecting you."

"Nicholas, unless Xandie has been recognized incompetent, which I know she hasn't, then what you've done can be misconstrued as fraud." Winifred shot a glance at Chief Braun who smiled at Nicholas Meyers.

"It wasn't like that at all. I'm helping my daughter."

Xandie took a deep breath and stepped out from behind the desk. She strode straight to the mayor and snatched the contract, proceeding to rip it in half. *Take that, puny arm muscles.* She stood with her hands on her hips. "Let me be clear to my father, Mr. Mitas, Mr. Mayor and all residents of Point Muse. *I. Am. Not. Selling.* I'm staying, so deal with it if you want access to the library." She stomped back to Winifred and her chair.

Clapping reverberated around the room. Harrows, all shapes and sizes, stood in the last few rows of chairs in the room. All hollering for Xandie. Her family, at least the one from Point Muse, was overjoyed she was staying.

"Mr. Mayor, I think the complaints have been defended and rebutted splendidly, don't you?" Winifred arched a brow at the mayor.

With a slap of his hand on the desk, the mayor yelled over the clamor. "All complaints are dismissed. Alexandra Meyers has met requirements and suitability for the inheritance of Sera Meyers' estate. Land, library and feline included. This matter is closed." The mayor stood and shook off Irene's hand as she tried to pull him aside and whisper.

Chief Braun, his mother, Aggie and deputy sister marched past Xandie with high-fives.

Braun spoke to her for a moment. "I know you have that receipt. It won't take long to pry the information out of Lila or Holly. In the meantime, stay safe and avoid any more murders." He quirked an eyebrow at Xandie and smirked, blue eyes twinkling.

She fought a corresponding quiver. *No quiver.* None for Zach *'burr-in-the-rear-end'* Braun. None. "I'll try my best, Chief Braun." Xandie swept into a tide of well-wishers.

It was over; she got to keep Theo and the library. She had a home and family. It was all done except for one fact.

There was still a killer out there hunting her…

NINE

Lila wrapped Xandie in a bear hug as she escaped into Lila's bakery. "Wahoo. You get to stay unless a maniac kills you. But don't worry, we'd get some witch to resurrect you as a flesh-eating zombie librarian if that happens. It's a win-win situation."

Xandie extricated herself from Lila's freaky version of smothering. "Thanks, I think."

Lila led Xandie to a vacant table and forced her down. "Sit. Hot chocolate and a feast of butter puffs coming your way." She bustled off, a hive of frenetic energy.

"She means well, but sugared energy has to go somewhere else other than her hips."

"Mom, I can feel you being mean," Lila sang from the counter.

Amelia rolled her eyes and her sister, Winifred, snickered.

"Well, dear. It's good to see you trouble-free for the moment." Winifred smiled, but it soon faded. "I'm sorry about your father but he was always a poop head."

Amelia agreed with her sister. "We never understood why your mother adored him. But I guess he canceled out the Harrow craziness, at least for a while."

"I can't believe he tried to pull this on me. But then again, it's a classic Nicholas Meyers' move. Same move he pulls in the library when he wants something." Xandie slumped in the chair, exhausted.

Lila dumped a huge pile of butter puffs in front of Xandie, along with a large cup of steaming hot chocolate. "Never mind. You have the library and us now. And you have a sugar coma right in front of you."

Xandie chuckled. "You're right." She grabbed a puff and chomped down, moaning as the sugar hit her system. She mumbled around a mouthful, "Where's Holly?"

Winifred wrinkled her nose. "That strange Harrow aberration of mine is haunting the morgue to get a feel for dead people's auras."

Xandie spat a trail of crumbs out on the table as she dislodged a lump of food out of her windpipe. "I can't imagine her in the morgue."

"Part of her father's training. Makes her more open to interpreting the signs in the visions she's given in relation to death. She hasn't found a family to bind to yet, so she gets general warnings for those around her." Winifred amended her words. "Some people around her. She's coming into her powers later than normal. She's unpredictable right now."

"It would've been much easier if she'd inherited the Harrow earth magic, but at least she isn't boring." Amelia poked Winifred in the side. "Come on, old girl, I need your help with a constipated tabby."

Winifred shuddered. "Can't wait." She buzzed a kiss on Xandie's forehead. "Be careful and don't guzzle too much sugar or you'll have nightmares."

Waving goodbye to aunts, Xandie closed her eyes and sipped her rich hot chocolate.

"I was just trying to help. This place is toxic. I was protecting you. You don't understand."

Xandie cracked her eyes open and squinted. Her father stood next to the table, his tie askew. The uptight, fastidious Nicholas Meyers. This meant he was in full meltdown mode. "This place isn't toxic for me. I'm meant to be here and I'm not you. I like Point Muse. I have friends and cousins here."

Her father grabbed his tie and twisted it back into place. "I don't understand your misplaced emotional attachment, but I will be there for you when you need a place to run to." Her father spun and stalked to the door without a backward glance.

"I am so grateful I have the Harrows," Xandie mumbled into her hot chocolate as she set about worshipping its sugary goodness uninterrupted. Her father couldn't help the way he was; her mother's disappearance had changed him for the worse. Mom always softened him. But Xandie was through obeying. Point Muse, the library, and her sarcastic feline were her future.

"Sorry for the kerfuffle today." Nigel Cummings slid into the chair next to Xandie and smiled sheepishly.

Sighing, Xandie nodded, not willing to put her drink down on the off chance he might leave. "It's fine, Mr. Mayor. It's over now, both the murder charge and my father's attempt at helping me."

"Of course. I just wanted to make sure there were no hard feelings with me presiding over the decision et cetera."

"Part of your job, I guess. I'm glad it ended well.

Although there are a few people, including your sister, who weren't too pleased."

Cummings waved her words away. "Irene likes rules and abhors chaos. Everything must be straight and narrow, no deviations. Her temper sometimes gets the better of her. Just ignore her grumpiness."

"Sounds like my father. Maybe we should set them up?" Xandie smothered her snort. That would be a scary combination.

"Irene's all about the job. She's my father's son. More than I am. He always wanted her in the family business. But he died, and she moved in with me."

Family job? "Administration or politics?"

"Bit of both. She has the spine for it, but no patience. So here I am, the mayor of Point Muse." He stood and extended his hand for a shake.

Xandie tried to place her cup down but missed the table and the contents splashed all over his extended hand. "I'm so sorry. Please, let me..." She grabbed napkins and mopped the mass of hot chocolate from his hand. Thankfully, it had cooled enough to not burn.

"No, no. It's an accident. No need to worry."

"It is my fault. I'm a natural klutz." Xandie grabbed the mayor's hand and taking care, wiped his ring. It looked like an old antique with Latin engraved around the outside and symbols edged in red inside.

The mayor yanked his hand away, looking embarrassed at her attention.

"I hope I haven't ruined your ring. It looks like an antique."

He jerked before forcing a laugh. "This? It's too solid to be ruined. My father gave it to me, it passes down from father to son."

"Oh, okay. Still hope I didn't ruin it."

He kept his hand with the ring behind his back and out of Xandie's view. "All good, I promise. Now, I must get going. I need to calm... err, speak to my sister. I'll see you later." The mayor sidled out of the bakery, keeping his hand hidden.

"What's up with that?" Xandie pondered on his weird behavior. He acted like he was hiding his hand from her. She clicked her fingers—or *hiding his ring.* "Lila," Xandie called out and rushed to the bakery counter. She leaned over, looking for her cousin.

"Why are you hanging over my counter?" Lila popped up right behind Xandie and scared her enough she nearly toppled right over. Grabbing the back of Xandie's shirt, Lila tugged her back.

Xandie spun and shook her cousin. "Quick, I need paper and a pencil."

"Wow, pushy much?" Lila grabbed a notepad and pen from the counter and shoved them at Xandie. "Is this a normal freak-out for you?"

Drawing a symbol on the paper, she showed it to Lila. "This was on the mayor's ring. I spilled a drink on him and got a look at it when I cleaned him up."

"So, you're clumsy and you like jewelry on men. Why so worked up?"

"It's the symbol. I've seen it before. I think it's in the library. I need to get back and check it out. But it feels important." Xandie knew she'd seen it before. She'd come across it in her shelving somewhere. "Does the family have any special supernatural flavor?"

"As far as I know they're both plain old humans, but I think I heard a rumor or two they might have a warrior as a descendant. But I'm not sure. Ask Theo or the library. They're the experts."

Nodding her thanks, Xandie waved goodbye to Lila and left. "I need to get back to the library pronto and give Theo the good news."

Was talking to herself insanity? At least no one was around to report her to the council. Otherwise she'd be back in court in a flash.

"Good thing I'm here to oblige," stated a voice behind her. "At the same time, we can discuss where the receipt is from Aaron's garage. The one for a broken taillight for a green SUV?"

Almost no one. Zach Braun, bear shifter extraordinaire, closes in for the kill.

"I'm sure I'll be fine walking back, Chief Braun. My stalker won't want to pay to get the car fixed again so soon after their last tangle with me."

"Nope, I insist." Zach opened the car door and waved her in.

With no way to get out gracefully, Xandie gave in and slouched into the seat. Braun was about to grill her; she felt the flames already.

Starting the car, Braun navigated out of Point Muse, heading toward Xandie's house. "Give me the receipt now and I don't send you back to jail for impeding an investigation?"

"Fine," Xandie huffed. "No point hiding it." She grabbed the receipt out of her bra and laid it on the seat next to Braun. "There you go. I must have accidentally picked this up at the garage this morning.

Braun snorted. "When Holly had her traumatic tomato ketchup injury?"

Xandie winced. Put like that the whole incident looked a tad stupid and dangerous. "Holly caved, didn't she?" The morgue was in the building next door to the police station and council chambers.

Braun knew exactly what weak link to hit to get the information.

"Melted like a marshmallow. She could never keep a secret from me. I used to babysit her and my sister. I've known her for a long time. So, give me the details of the receipt."

Rolling her eyes, Xandie grabbed the receipt and read it out. "One taillight cracked in a green SUV. Car leased to the Council. Paid by cash, council employee."

"Who does the car belong to? Who paid for it?"

"Paid in cash, no name council employee. Could have been anyone taking it in for repairs. There's a note the SUV is for council use only. That's it." The mayor looked better and better for the killer. Especially if she found information in the library about the ring. Might make his reasons for murder clear.

"Plenty of people who work for the council."

Xandie curled her lip. And he called himself an investigator. "Pretty sure a certain level of employee would only use this vehicle. I'm betting the number of people who drove it would be small."

"And also, none of your business since you aren't law enforcement. Stay out of this mess and away from Aaron and his garage too." Braun pulled up in Xandie's driveway and sat in the car with the engine running. "I'll wait here until you give me the all clear."

"You know it's safe here, the library protects its own."

"Didn't protect your lawyer."

"He wasn't the library's. But I get your point." Xandie exited the car, unlocked her front door and peered around. Theo snoozed on the couch and she doubted he'd be calm if they had an intruder. She gave the thumbs up to Braun and he flashed his lights in response before heading off down the driveway.

Xandie leaned against the door and breathed in and out. Peace, at least for the moment. Or until she tracked down the killer. Speaking of the killer, she had a symbol to track down, but first a good strong cup of tea to balance her sugary overdose from earlier. She brewed a pot of Earl Gray and entered the library, ornate teacup in hand. She ducked just in time as a heavy scroll flew toward her. Another four scrolls fenced each other in the corner of the room and a pile of heavy tomes had arranged themselves like dominoes about to fall.

"What's going on here?" Xandie swerved, as the dueling scrolls zoomed too close to her head for comfort. Tea sloshed in her teacup and Xandie placed the cup on her desk for safety. A loud bang above her head had her eyeing the ceiling worriedly. Instead of a hole and plaster falling on her, hundreds of little gold fairy lights twinkled on the ceiling like stars. "What's up, library? This is manic even for you."

"It's trying to celebrate your win at the Council meeting and the fact you're no longer a murder suspect." Theo slunk past, swerving at the last minute before collapsing on Xandie's feet.

The lights on the ceiling now took on a frenetic disco pace of twinkling.

Weird, but thoughtful. "Thanks, library. I'm happy to be here too." She snatched the drawing she'd made at Lila's bakery from her purse and held it up in the air. "Library, have you seen the symbol before?"

The twinkling lights froze and then winked out of existence one by one. The dueling scrolls dropped to the floor and the domino books fell backward onto the floor.

"Buzzkill." Theo rolled off Xandie's feet and vomited a fur ball, just missing her boots.

"Why? What's wrong with the symbol?"

A scroll flew from a shelf to fall into Xandie's hand. She unrolled it and right in the middle of the document was the same symbol as the mayor's ring.

She read the Latin from the outside of a seal. "Equis. Pura. Sanguis." Xandie shuddered when she realized human skulls were engraved on the seal. In the center of the symbol was a bleeding red Templar cross. Superimposed over it was an upside-down triangle with lines and dots through the middle.

"Knights of the Pure Blood. Sanguis knights. The skulls represent humanity, the cross represents their beginnings with the Templars and the upside-down triangle is the alchemical symbol for blood. Why did you draw this?" Theo backed away from the drawing.

"In Lila's bakery. I spilled drink over the mayor's hand and when I mopped it up, I spotted the ring. Struck me as important so I copied the symbol down."

"The ring passes from father to son as does the training. If the mayor of Point Muse has that ring, then he's a knight of Sanguis...*and your killer*. He must have targeted Sera for the library and the other victims because they're descended from supernaturals." Theo arched his back and fluffed his fur until he resembled a giant black yarn ball with eyes.

Xandie slapped the drawing on the desk. Her tea surged over the top of the cup and pooled on the timber. "I knew it. I knew our killer was the mayor.

He wanted the library and had access to Sera at the council meeting. Cummings owns the building where the police found the agent and he was at my house when the lawyer died. He's the Knight. What do I do now?"

"You tell Braun and let him deal with it. It's his job."

Xandie shook her head. "He'll never believe it's the mayor. A pillar of the community? No, I need to speak to the girls and work out how to track and expose him."

Theo blinked his cat eyes in disgust. "Xandie, that's a horrible idea. Stay away from him. Go hide and let Braun take him down."

Nibbling her lip, she paced the library. "Sera, Louise Maker and Mr. Essam were all killed, not me. I think he's removing all barriers to his access of the land and the library. It would be too obvious to take me out now. I'll be the last to go. That poor banker, Mr. Mitas, might be next."

"Mitas. What a hack," Theo snorted.

"What's wrong with Mitas?"

"Once upon a time, his descendants were filthy rich, all wanted by the world for their gifts. Now all George has is a lust for gold and no gift to make it."

"He has a supernatural need to collect gold?"

"He's descended from King Midas. So that's pretty much it."

"Another supernatural. Exactly the mayor's modus operandi. The banker's next, we have to warn him." Xandie grabbed her phone and googled the banker's phone number. Thankfully, both the Internet and phone reception were working.

"That would be you, not we. Remember?" Theo pointed a paw to his mouth.

"Fine," she mouthed as she tapped the number in and waited for someone to speak "Mr. Mitas, I know it sounds weird, but I have to warn you."

"Who is this?"

"Xandie Meyers. I think someone will kill you. You need to get somewhere safe."

"*Librarian*, leave me alone. In fact, I'm calling the Chief right now to tell him you threatened me."

"No, please. This is important," Xandie pleaded with the man, but he ignored her and hung up. "No gratitude there. I tried to save his life, now he's reporting me to Braun. I can't win." Frustrated, Xandie picked her teacup up and sipped. "Blech." She spat the bitter-tasting liquid out. The tea annihilated her taste buds. She dumped the cup onto the table. "Did you cough a fur ball into my tea?"

"Do I look like someone who vomits on

command? What's wrong with it?" Theo jumped up on the desk and sniffed. He drew back with a revolted expression. "It's curdled. Gone off."

"But that's fresh milk. It can't be curdled."

"Hang on." Theo took a running leap and flew, landing close to a shelf in a perfect ten-point jump. He shot his paw out and grabbed something that let out a high-pitched shriek, which threatened to burst her eardrums. Theo batted the figure around, only to let it escape toward Xandie.

Thinking it a mouse she leaped onto the chair, squealing.

Theo pounced again and bit the creature in half, spitting the head out like unwanted prey. "Imps. Hate those dirty hell-spawn." The gray headless body wiggled for a moment before dissolving into ash.

"What in all hells is that?" Xandie pointed trembling finger at the pile of gray ash on the library floor.

"Exactly. Hell." Theo pushed the pile around and sneezed a cloud of ash into the air.

She waved her hands around her head to neutralize the dead imp particles around her.

The library helpfully dropped a book titled the *'Denizens of Hell and What They Can Do for You'* on Xandie's toes. Bellowing, she grabbed the book and danced around in agony. Pain subsided until only a dull throb remained. She limped to a chair, checked for gray ash or reconstituted imp and collapsed in relief. "I repeat. What was that thing you slaughtered and then blew in my face?"

"An imp, and where there's one, there's always more. They're annoying pack animals from Hell that do nothing but cause chaos. Vermin. They're worse than dogs." Theo nosed around the library floor, hunting for more.

Xandie flipped open the book the library had dropped on her foot and read a passage. "Imps are the lowest denizens of the demonic hierarchy. Normally employed in mischievous and devious acts and love nothing more than annoying stray humans. They crave attention and are creatures of impulse unless under control of a stronger demon or master. Imps are both satanic minions and attention seeking pranksters. In appearance, most imps can reach the size of a mouse or a large rat. With demonic interference they can grow to the size of a small dog." Xandie gagged but kept on reading.

"They are colorless and genderless, and bony with pointed ears, teeth and tail. Their faces are frozen in a grimace or evil smirk. Elder imps will grow a small set of horns; this is a mark of importance. Imps will have small nubs for horns. They travel in packs and can congregate in large numbers and are used by a demon or human master to flush victims or targets out. One imp is an annoyance; a pack of imps can be compared to a plague of rats or human toddlers. Always call an imp exterminator to deal with them."

She had imps. Grey horrible plague animals from hell. Just when she thought Point Muse couldn't surprise her, along came hairless residents of hell. "Know any imp exterminators, Theo?" Xandie frowned when he refused to answer except for a thin wail from deep inside the house. Bolting out of a chair in search of Theo, Xandie locked the door to the library, but kept hold of a book. It made a handy imp-flattening device.

Xandie poked her head around the corner of the hallway, facing the sitting room and the stairs. The noise of a hundred tiny little claws tapping on the floor hit her first. Little gray, hairless bodies ran every which way. Including the four attached to Theo as he galloped past. One imp hung on the cat's tail and flapped in the air like a flag. The other two dotted along his spine. The fourth one attached between Theo's ears, hanging onto the cat's pointed appendages and trying to drive.

"Help me. I swear I will never vomit fur balls on your pillow again," Theo screamed as he zoomed past her.

"Wait, what? That's disgusting."

"Help me." Theo's wailing voice faded as the imps drove him into the kitchen.

A scratching of claws above her had Xandie eyeing the roof. But instead of frolicking imps, parachuting ones confronted her instead.

Parachuting. With. Her. Bras.

An imp with her favorite lilac bra in hand poised on the balustrade above. Other imps below chanted an incomprehensible name. Giggling, he raised his tiny little claws and hoisted Xandie's bra above his head. He bent his gray, hairless knees and launched himself into space. His round gargoyle-like face twisted into a smirk. With the bra stretched overhead, he plummeted like a rock to the ground and hit with a spectacular spray of ash.

"Oh, heck, no. No more suicide by underwear. Especially mine." She ran to the kitchen and surprised a gruesome gaggle of imps about to boomerang a paring knife at Theo, who lay bound and gagged with kitchen tea towels. Xandie used her thick book as an imp battering ram until she reached Theo. She grabbed him, still bound, under her other arm and bolted out the front door. Chest heaving and cat in tow, Xandie stumbled away from her door and called Lila. It wasn't too long before her cousin sped up the driveway, a white van in tow.

"War zone in there, huh?" Lila pointed to the ash decorating Xandie's white T-shirt and Theo's black fur. Xandie shuddered and shook both of them out. The library's book on imps hit the ground with a thud. "I forgot I had the book when I grabbed Theo. Must've captured a stray imp and squished it when we ran outside."

A trio of men in HAZMAT suits with tanks and sprayers on their backs shambled into the house.

"Come on, sweetie. Let's get you and Theo to my apartment and settled in with pizza. They should be done late tonight, and you can return triumphant tomorrow."

"Who are they?" Xandie let Lila tow her and Theo to the car.

"Special kind of cleaners. Zach uses them when they have any supernatural infestations. They fill the tanks with holy water. The imps will dust in a heartbeat and even better, these guys clean up afterward. You'll have a sparkling, imp free house in no time." Lila buckled Xandie in like a child and deposited Theo on the back seat. "It's good timing anyway.

Mom came around with a box of your mom's stuff she left behind. You can have pizza with me and have a look."

Everything seemed such a muddle in Point Muse, but at least she had family looking out for her. Xandie shifted back in her seat, wondering what answers she wanted more.

The killers' identity or her mother's? Because right now both were a complete mystery to her.

TEN

Theo purred as he snuggled against an imp-free Xandie. She'd had to wash her hair three times before *eau du imp* disappeared. Now she'd had a feast of pizza and way too many of Lila's cupcakes. Sugar equaled happiness in this town.

"Here you go. I've no clue what's in it." Lila dropped a cardboard box decorated with pictures of pink houses next to Xandie on the couch. She waited for Xandie to open the package.

Xandie extended a hand and traced her mother's handwritten name on the side of the box. "My mother wrote this."

"Yep, her best memories went into the box. Miranda didn't take it with her when you all left, but she updated it every time she visited. Mom says it's crammed full of stuff."

Her mom stored her memories in Point Muse instead of leaving them with her dad. Maybe she'd thought dad would throw them out? Or had she planned to bring Xandie back to town permanently? So many questions, including why and how her mother had disappeared, ran through her mind. She slid a finger under the lid and let it fall off the other side. It was jam-packed full of stuffed toys, ribbons and trophies, photos and even a drawing Xandie had done as a child. "Look, Lila." She held up a drawing of a cat chasing fairies. "It's Theo, and I drew him chasing fairies."

"He loves tormenting them. He hasn't done it in a while. I think he's too fat for it now."

Theo opened one eye. "I think you're overdosing on your own products. Maybe sugar-free is the way to go."

"Shush, feline, no mean comments when you're in my domain." Lila flicked a strawberry from one of the leftover cupcakes at Theo.

"How did you know what he said? So far I'm the only one who can hear him."

"His face. He gets this expression. I call it the *aren't-we-glad-we-can't-hear-him* face. And don't let him fool you, he decides who hears him. He just likes being a pain."

Rummaging through the box, Xandie grabbed a floppy bunny with only one ear. "This was Mom's. I remember her talking about a one-eared pirate bunny."

Lila chuckled. "Mom used to tell me stories about a one-eyed pirate fairy when I was little. There's a theme happening."

A photo snagged Xandie's attention. One of all the sisters together. "Look how young they are." She showed the picture to her cousin.

"Aunt Win would have been fourteen, mom fifteen and your mom almost seventeen. Check out the curly brown hair. Mom so dyes her hair. She swears that shade of reddish-brown is natural...liar."

Xandie giggled. All the women had wild brown hair. The sisters were striking. She found another picture of her mom with her arms around a man. Her young-looking father, no silver streaks in this photo. Only big smiles and an even larger tummy on her mother. She must have been pregnant with Xandie. Who knew only a few years later the family would shatter with her mom's disappearance?

"It's okay to grieve, Xandie. Your mom loved you. You're entitled to have sad times, especially when you're looking through photos." Lila patted Xandie's head as she walked past. "I have a new cupcake mix and you're my test subject. Blueberry and cilantro. See what you think?"

Hazard of having a baker for a cousin. Weird concoctions of food tested on your stomach lining. Xandie reached into the box and drew out another photo. This one didn't provoke happy memories. A photo of a mom's car after she disappeared. Windows down, doors open. Her mom's purse open on the seat and her phone out, but not on. This must be a crime scene photo. Someone had slipped it into her mother's box. She hadn't seen it before, but she'd been told the car engine had been running and the radio left blaring.

A lump formed in her throat and she cleared it twice with a cough. She couldn't remember anything of that day except for the odd flash. An image of a mom arguing with Sera. Of her cuddling with Theo in the library. Then a flash of mom bending over her, telling her to stay safe. And then nothing. Just a complete blank.

"Your mom's car after she disappeared?" Lila placed a plate of cakes on the table and sat next to Xandie.

"Yeah. Looks like it was taken right after they

found the car, just after sunset. Cops found me wandering an hour later. Miles away from the car. It was almost winter, and the frosts had set in, so I was near frozen. I wasn't talking except when they took me to Sera and all I kept repeating was Theo's name. My father picked me up hours later. Drove me straight to a therapist and refused to talk about my mother for years."

Lila pried the photo out of Xandie's hand. She frowned for a moment before speaking. "There were no signs of struggle or any hint someone had hurt her, right?"

"Nothing. They decided she must've had a mental breakdown and walked away. We were near the coast, so the police thought she had gone over a cliff somewhere. That's why we never found her."

"I don't think she had a nervous breakdown."

"Why not? My father sure did. He blames Point Muse and Sera for her death."

Lila pointed to the frosted windows in the picture of the vehicle. "Because of that."

Xandie leaned in. People found her mom's car quickly after she disappeared. The photo showed fogged-up windows. Even with the open doors, with the motor running, the interior would have been warmer than the frigid air outside. Hence the degree of condensation. And right where Lila pointed was a symbol drawn onto the fogged window on the driver's side. "What's that?"

Lila jumped up and rummaged through a drawer, triumphantly holding aloft a kid's magnifying glass. "Try this."

She threw the magnifying glass across the room. Xandie snatched it out of the air and peered at the photo. She drew in a swift breath as she focused on the symbol.

"What is it?" Lila crowded in next to Xandie.

Xandie tapped at the photo with the tip of one finger. "Remember the symbol? The one I drew of the mayor's ring that the library identified as the Knights of Pure Blood? This is the same design."

"Knights took Aunt Miranda?"

"Why else would she draw that symbol on the car window? She must have known what was happening. She sent me away and stayed behind to distract them." Her mom hadn't walked away from her and her father. Someone had made her do it.

"If we find this knight, do we find who took your mother? Could she still be alive?"

Xandie licked her lips. Thinking of her mom alive and with them again almost overwhelmed her synapses. But she couldn't let hope build, not after so many years apart. "She can't be alive after this long, otherwise she'd have made it back to us. But maybe we can find out what happened."

"This is getting serious. Should we get Mom and Aunt Winifred in on this too?"

"I think that's a good idea. We need to find the killer before someone else gets hurt."

Maybe someone just like her.

"You do this every day?" Xandie wiped the sweat off her forehead and went back to kneading bread.

Lila piped icing on a tray of little cakes. "You want your butter puffs? You need to put in the sweat for them."

"I'm rethinking my addiction."

Lila giggled. "At least your house is now free of demonic squatters. Theo doesn't need to live in fear of his fur."

Thanks to those cleaners. Xandie shuddered. "Those ugly little things were nasty. Thanks for putting me up for the night."

"Getting the bread kneaded before the lunch rush is thanks enough."

One of Lila's employees poked her head around

the door of the kitchen. "There's a phone call for Xandie at the front counter."

"Saved by the bell." Xandie smirked and cleaned off her doughy hands. Ignoring Lila's growl, she slipped through the kitchen doors and grabbed the phone. Thankfully it wasn't busy yet, so the lunchtime rush hadn't begun. Only a few diehard customers inhaling an early feed were present. "Xandie Meyers."

"I swear you're a trouble magnet."

Zach Braun's sigh at the end of his words tickled Xandie's ear. "Those imps were nothing to do with me."

"Did you at least set up a watch on the house and the library?"

"Aunt Winifred and some of her friends are keeping an eye out. Not to mention the other nosy gossips out there."

"The dragon shifters. They always like to know what's going on in town. For some of them, knowledge is gold."

"Yeah. A teenage dragon visited the library before the council meeting to tell me they were watching and judging my performance."

"That's dragons for you. So, the cleaners worked? Any idea who set them on your house?"

Xandie leaned against the counter, keeping an eye on the customers. Last problem she needed was a customer coming in for coffee and leaving with gossip. She noticed a man hunched over in the corner. Mr. Mitas, the banker, hunkered over a golden cranberry and ginseng muffin. He'd wandered in earlier and sneered at Xandie behind the counter.

"Xandie?"

She realized she'd stopped talking while she stared at Mr. Mitas. "Sorry, I'm helping Lila out of the bakery as thanks for putting me up the last night."

"Is there anything else you need to tell me? Anything? You have a habit of hiding important information and then someone dies."

He wasn't wrong about that. Too many corpses with a link to her had surfaced lately. Braun probably had indigestion at the thought of her working near food with her bad luck. He already knew about the SUV lease to the Council. But she should at least give him a heads up about the Sanguis Knight.

"I have some information that might interest you. I found a photo in my mother's stuff. A crime scene photo taken after she disappeared." Xandie focused on Mr. Mitas, trying to distract herself from the image of a deserted car and the symbol drawn on the window. The banker shifted on his chair. He shoved an empty plate to the side of the table and rubbed his stomach, wincing.

"What's wrong with the photo?"

"A symbol's drawn into the foggy windows of my mom's car. A symbol for the Knights Sanguis."

"Pure Blood killers, you mean. You think they're connected to your mom's disappearance?"

"Maybe, but I've seen the same symbol here in Point Muse."

The banker shoved his table aside and vomited on the floor.

"Where did you see it?"

Eew. Lila would hate the mess. Mr. Mitas started to writhe on his chair, white liquid pooling in the corners of his mouth. "Oh. My. Goodness." Did the banker have rabies?

"Xandie, what's wrong?"

The man keeled over and fell from his chair, twitching spasmodically until his body froze. Xandie stared, shocked. "You need to get an ambulance here right away."

"What's happened now?"

The few customers in the shop crowded around Mr. Mitas, trying to get a response out of him.

Xandie moved the phone away from her mouth and hollered for her cousin.

"Alexandra Meyers, what's going on?" Braun yelled down the line.

"You need to get here ASAP. I think George Mitas just died." Xandie slammed the phone down. She knew in her bones his death by golden cranberry muffin would be laid at her door.

Her bad luck still held firm.

"You're closed until the health inspector can check your bakery out."

Xandie wrapped an arm around her devastated cousin, and Holly on the other side did the same, both girls keeping Lila propped upright.

"I don't understand. All the ingredients are natural and sourced locally. I adhere to all health regulations." Lila shook her head in shock.

"That may be the problem, natural ingredients. Maybe you picked the wrong ones?"

"No way. I know what I'm doing. He's the only regular who eats my golden cranberry and ginseng muffin. I take extra care with it and always have his serving of muffin put aside."

"Sorry, Lila. The health inspector is already on the way. I've got Caleb rushing the sample over for testing himself. We'll have an answer soon. Meanwhile, take a rest. All of you." He pinned Xandie with an impressive stare. "No more investigating. I've got it from here."

All the girls nodded as he left, taking his personnel with him.

"This is my fault, isn't it? They couldn't frame me, now they've moved on to my friends and family." Xandie squeezed Lila's arm. "I'm sorry."

Lila shook off the girls' hugs and pointed to the ceiling. "Coffee and cake upstairs in my apartment. And don't worry. I'll try not to poison you." She stomped up the stairs, with a worried Holly and Xandie close behind.

Lila banged plates in the kitchen and dumped a rich chocolate cake on the table with a pot of coffee.

Xandie and Holly both tucked in. Easy-going Lila disappeared only to be replaced by grumpy cook and witch.

"It's not your fault, Xandie." Lila took a sip of her coffee. "The killer is the one to blame, not you. We'll track him down and my bakery will reopen." She glared at her cousins. "Got it?"

Xandie nodded. "How do you think Mr. Mitas

died?"

"Poison," Holly matter-of-factly stated. "Obvious with the frothing mouth, vomiting, and convulsions."

Lila stared. "Sometimes you scare me. Quiet little mouse to poison expert in a heartbeat."

"Not expert, but I've seen it in the morgue. Whatever he ate poisoned him."

"But I served that muffin twenty minutes before he died. Why didn't it work straight away?"

"Because someone exchanged the ginseng for water hemlock." Aunt Winifred stood in the doorway, along with a wrinkled old woman with lavender streaks in her short hair. Lila's mother crowded in behind them.

The wrinkled old woman in a snazzy emerald-jogging suit beamed a wrinkled smile and crossed to Xandie. "My sweet granddaughter. You look just like your mother." She gripped both of Xandie's cheeks and pinched. "All my girls are beautiful. Single, but beautiful."

"Okay?" Xandie tried to mumble through cheeks full of old women fingers.

"Goodness sakes, Mom. Let the poor girl breathe. We're here about murder, remember?"

Amelia pried her mother away and pushed her into a single chair next to Xandie. "Xandie, this is your grandmother, Elspeth. She's been away at a yoga retreat. She's our plant and herb expert."

"They found me at the hairdresser's getting my purple highlight touched up." Elspeth patted her streaked coif. "Now if you want to know anything about the town, go there. But I'd be careful, the girls hold a grudge and they ain't happy with getting booted from your property."

"I should trust my hair to annoyed hairdressers with a grudge?"

Her grandmother waved Xandie's comment away. "They wouldn't dare go against me. But it wouldn't hurt to apologize and offer your land up for their rituals." Grandma Elspeth winked at Xandie and clapped her hands. "Right, we were talking about murder, weren't we?"

Wouldn't hurt to mend some naked fences. They were the only hairdressers in town. Who knows what juicy gossip they had about Point Muse and the murders? "Fine. I'll do it," Xandie interrupted the murder babble.

"Good girl." Elspeth patted Xandie on the knee. "Now, death girl is right. It was poison. They substituted water hemlock for the ginseng. A sweet muffin hid the bitter taste. It would have been the only way the killer could get that idiot to eat it."

"First, that idiot was a regular and second, I keep my powdered ginseng in a container in my walk-in pantry. Away from all my other ingredients. I'm in and out all day but anyone could have exchanged it for hemlock. But why frame me?"

"We think the target's still Xandie. Pure good luck she was working on the same day Mitas died. The goal is framing Xandie, not you, Lila. You're just collateral damage." Winifred exchanged a look with her sister, Amelia.

"Why would the killer want to frame me? I was just there because of the imps, so what's my link to the victim? Aside from the obvious." She rolled her eyes. Yeah, let's just discount the fact the victim wanted the estate's land and Xandie had rung the night before to warn him of danger.

"Because the only available water hemlock in the area grows around the pond on your land, my darling." Elspeth frowned. "They must be residents of Point Muse, to know that. Plus, they'd have to have expertise or knowledge to harvest it."

Holly weighed in. "But you said it was good luck on the killer's part Xandie was here. Wouldn't the killer control the imps?"

"Not necessarily, but those particular imps that invaded the library strictly belong to its demon master. He'd love to get his hands on the library. Speaking of hands on..." Elspeth giggled and fanned her face. "Such a lovely body he has now. He's mellowed over the centuries, although he's still scheming to get inside. But I don't think even he would commit murder now."

The clamor of all three cousins caused Elspeth to clamp hands over her ears. "For goodness sakes, what is this generation coming to if they can't spot a demon on the earthly plane?" She scoured her daughters with beady eyes. "I blame the hippie generation, they never paid attention to their lessons. It was all about the weed and the orgy sex."

Amelia and Winifred looked appalled and hustled Elspeth out.

Elspeth yelled over a shoulder at Xandie, "Check the charming professor out and don't forget the hairdressers."

The three women squabbled all the way down the stairs and outside. Lila opened the window and peered out. "They're still fighting." She kept up a running commentary on the arguments outside. "Elspeth just stuck a foot out and tripped mom. But mom grabbed Aunt Winifred, and now they're both lying on the ground. Grandma Elspeth's on the run and headed into the lingerie shop across the road."

Xandie shuddered at the image of the wrinkled purple-haired grandmother parading around in black lace. "Do we want to know why she's in a sexy underwear shop?"

Holly frantically shook her head. "No pictures, no pictures in my head."

Lila shut the window. "She's having a fling with the owner of the flower shop down the road. Mom has walked in on them a few times. I think Elspeth keeps him supplied with go-go juice, if you know what I mean. They've broken her bed twice now."

Xandie tried to get back on track. "Hemlock? The professor is a Demon?" Anything to get the picture of a broken bed and pensioners out of her head.

"Elspeth has had a few dealings with them, but mostly they give her a wide berth. I've never met any. How about you, Holly?"

"I met a few. Some are okay. Depends what they want."

Xandie would never get used to the casual way Point Muse residents had of announcing the weird. Then again...she remembered the way red light flickered in the professor's eyes when she'd run into him. Right around the time people discovered Louise Maker's body. Maybe the idea wasn't so outlandish.

"Hanging around a morgue you see weird stuff. Calling death can sometimes attract darker things like demons," Holly stated.

"Wow, I have to re-evaluate you and your life. You're much more interesting than you look."

Holly poked a tongue out at Lila. "In that case I should mention I have a new job now."

"Don't tell me you let Aunt Win drag you into her candle business? She'd drive you crazy in a day."

Xandie agreed with Lila. Her aunt was lovely, but spending a day discussing different candles' healing properties would drive *her* crazy, let alone Winifred's own daughter.

"I'm not suicidal. No, since I've been training at the morgue, the coroner, who owns the Elysian Fields Funeral Home with his sister, offered me a job."

Dead silence met Holly's words. Xandie peeped at Lila, waiting to see her cousin's reaction to Holly's new job. She didn't have to wait long.

"Elspeth doesn't call you death girl for nothing. Provided you don't take your work home, who cares?" Lila snorted at her pun-worthy cleverness.

"Do you ever take anything seriously? This could be a good job for a training banshee." Holly frowned and crossed her arms.

Xandie intervened between the two cousins before a food fight began. "It's a good idea. Now can we get back to the murder, blood-thirsty knights, demons and what our next step is?"

Lila sneered at Holly. "Geez, lighten up. Making a joke in my black-hole of traumatic loss might have cheered me up."

Holly pointed to Xandie and ignored Lila. "Elspeth told us to focus on the Professor and the oldies at *'Here Today Gone Tomorrow'*. I'll see them tomorrow if you will?"

Nodding her agreement, Xandie turned to Lila. "What about you? Any ideas?"

"I'm betting the health inspector will be here tomorrow, so I'm hanging around here. But if I get spare time, I'll track down Elspeth for more information."

Xandie inhaled, held the breath deep in her lungs for a moment and then released it on a loud sigh. That was it. They had a plan. Her next step... suck up to octogenarian hairdressers who hated her. Get as much gossip as she could tolerate on the mayor, the professor and the murders. Easy. All she had to do was swallow her pride and invite old women to perform naked ceremonies on her land

Simple.

ELEVEN

Wrinkly leader number one, a.k.a. Olive Johnson, now with a beehive addition to her head, stood behind a black shiny counter. All purple hair highlights dissolved under the mass of red piled on top of her head. "You finally crossed our doorstep?"

Holly shoved Xandie further into the hairdressing salon. A surprisingly welcoming salon. Wood-framed mirrors on the walls, padded black leather chairs dotted around the room, small tables next to them. A bank of leather and black metal chairs faced mirrors. Sinks and massage chairs against the other wall, obscured by pinup girl-imaged room dividers. An ornate Victorian inspired chandelier hung in the center of the room. An effective use of an eclectic style that drew the customer in.

"If you finished cataloguing our style, what can I do for you?" Olive leaned on the counter and appraised Holly and Xandie. "Both of you have the Harrow hair, plain brown and straight. We can jazz it up and make you decent looking."

Xandie cleared her throat. "I'd like to offer an apology. Adapting to Point Muse has been a learning experience. If you and your group want to use my land, you can. I just need advance notice on the date and clothing state." *Apologetic enough to get a foot in the door?*

Olive's sister-in-law, Dorothy Johnson, sashayed up, leaned on the counter and sniffed dramatically. This time she sported a platinum blonde shaggy wig. "I suppose we can accept your condition. Sister, what do you think?"

Olive played with the red curl hanging down from her beehive and stared at Xandie's follicles. "Sounds fine, but I need to give you a trim of those split ends first. They offend me." Nodding to Dorothy, both women grabbed Xandie and Holly and shoved them into two chairs facing the mirrors.

Holly shook her shoulder length straight hair in protest. "I'm fine. Besides, I've never upset you. No need for follicle revenge."

"Traitor," Xandie hissed, but she fingered the

ends of her hair. Her hair was split and messy. She hadn't had a cut in months, and it showed. Her medium brown hair frizzed below her shoulders. Maybe she should try a new cut.

Olive clamped fingers on Xandie's head and forced it straight. "You need a trim and layers to get rid of the weight. What about colors? I have a lovely emerald highlight that would look fantastic on you."

"Ah, I'm fine with my color." Her mom's hair had been the same color before she disappeared.

Dorothy tittered, picking up a strand of Holly's limb hair. "No layers for you. How about a treatment and maybe a style cut? You have a great heart-shaped face."

Thinking for a moment, Holly agreed. "Do it. If it looks horrible, I'll unleash my grandmother on you."

Dorothy shuddered. "No need for nastiness. I don't know where you girls get your sass from."

Xandie and Holly looked at each other, muffling their giggles. If you wanted to survive the Harrows, sass was pretty much a requirement. Holly was the quiet one of the bunch and even she had a mouth on her.

"Seen any good murders?" Holly smiled sweetly as Dorothy gaped at her.

Talk about no tact. "My cousin meant isn't it horrible all these murders are happening? You heard the police cleared me of all the charges?" Xandie wanted subtle, not sledgehammer interview technique.

Olive slapped Xandie's shoulder. "Deal is we shampoo and then we dish on murder." She pointed to the washing station. "Now giddy up, girls, if you want the gossip."

Xandie shuffled to the basins and adjusted the awkward chair. Olive's fingers worked relaxation magic as she sloshed shampoo through Xandie's hair. Whatever the grievance she had with the naked group of wrinkled Wiccan practitioners, washing her hair wasn't one. From the snorting noises coming from Holly, she agreed. The sisters-in-law had a hair-dressing gift.

Finished with the wash, Olive led Xandie back to her seat. Dorothy and Holly trailed behind.

"Right, talk about any murders you want. But no comments on our hairdressing, got it, girlies?"

Agreeing in self-defense, because it never paid to anger somebody with scissors, Xandie wriggled in her chair, trying to work out how to how to bring up murders and suspects casually.

"Spit it out. We're unshakable in Point Muse...." Olive expertly snipped portions off Xandie's hair.

"Have you heard anything interesting around town?"

"You mean the murders? Or the steamy private lives of Point Muse residents?"

"Steamy?" Sidetracked, Xandie tried to picture a steamy situation. It wasn't pretty.

"You'd be surprised what people around here get up to." Olive sliced a long lock of hair and watched it plummet to the ground. "The professor causes heat. But not always the sexy kind."

Demon lord of Point Muse had groupies. What's the bet he was the same guy who'd burned the physical library down. "Hmmm," encouraged Xandie.

"Him and Sera used to squabble, but I think both kind of liked it. He dated that Aphrodite wannabe, Rose, but Aaron soon put a stop to that. Boy, I thought the Professor would flay Aaron right there at the Inn, but the Professor calmed down soon enough."

"The fight was about Rose?"

"No punches thrown, but I've never seen Aaron back down like that before. He swore afterward he'd seen flames in Amoru's eyes and then that same night he had a kitchen fire in that garage of his.

Maybe the guy's a lousy cook, but he swore he wasn't even cooking."

Made sense if Professor Amoru was the demon, he'd burned the library down once already with bale-fire. Why not a bachelor's kitchen? "Anything else about the mayor? Any goodies?"

Dorothy and Olive snorted in unison. Dorothy leaned over to Xandie. "Momma's boy? Or should we say sister's boy? He doesn't do squat without Irene's approval but he's protective of her too. Remember the council meeting?"

Olive agreed. "Talk about drama. Irene had a few dates with the Professor and Rose found out. *Meow*. Fur flew at that meeting night."

"Irene dated him too?" Xandie couldn't imagine the steel-spine spinster loosening up for date night moves.

"He dated both before he met Sera. Once he did, neither Rose nor Irene was good enough for him. But the mayor, he had it in for both Rose and Sera when he found out. Had words with Rose who was dating Aaron by then. But Sera laughed in his face. Wouldn't confirm or deny anything about her and the professor."

"What happened next?" This gossip was like a Days of Point Muse soap opera.

"The mayor went after Amoru. Accused him of using Irene. The mayor implied the professor wanted Sera's estate and courted her to get it. Amoru couldn't care less about the mayor. Told him he wasn't the one pulling the steel wool over the sheep's eyes. Mayor backed off and both he and his sister ignored the Professor. But the looks Irene gave Sera..." Rose shivered. "I don't know who hated her more, Irene or her brother."

Now wasn't that interesting? Once again, the Cummings involved in juicy gossip. Could the mayor have hated Sera enough to kill her? And what about the other murder? "And Maker, Essam and Mitas? Any issues I should know about?"

"Dorothy? You knew Louise better than me. Any gossip for our sleuths here?"

Dorothy pursed her lips. "She never dated Amoru but went out with the mayor a few times. She ended up ditching him though; she always thought he tried too hard. Too creepy for her. But I know the mayor wanted her to join some real estate deal, but she had already formed one with Essam and Mitas. She told him she wasn't interested. Next day he raised her rent and renovations started on her build-ing. She used to complain all the time about losing clients because of the noise."

More and more connections to the mayor and his sister. "When did the mayor and his sister move to Point Muse?"

"Twenty years ago, I guess. Irene was exactly the same, and the mayor had more hair and fewer products. They were quieter, less visible than they are now." Olive dragged her hairdryer out. "Now, fewer questions, more relaxing."

The drone of the hairdryer soothed Xandie and her eyes drooped. By the slumping of shoulders in Holly's chair, her cousin was as relaxed as she was. The slap on Xandie's shoulder was a shock to her system, and she sat bolt upright, eyes wide.

"What ya think?" Olive dusted the back of Xandie's neck and whipped the cape covering her off like a matador.

Xandie stared in the mirror. For a loud-mouth, naked Wicca-preforming octogenarian, she was a wizard with the scissors. Xandie's straight and lifeless brown hair now glowed a rich brown with gold highlights. Her hair fell down her back in a waterfall of waves. "Whoa, looks amazing."

"I'm good. Your great-aunt, unlike your Harrow aunts, never saw my hairdressing genius, but other members of your family are more appreciative."

Xandie looked over at Holly. A little elfin face

stared back at her. A sleek bob to her chin hung in sheets of golden brown. Holly twisted her head left and right.

"Looks fantastic, Holly."

Holly smiled and shook her head again. Every strand fell back into place with no effort. "Lila missed out for once."

Dorothy tittered. "Lila sneaks in every six weeks for a trim and treatment. Otherwise those curls would be frizz city. She inherited her father's hair. He has a curly mop. I guess it's all that humidity in the underworld."

"Sneaky cousin. She swore she'd never come here while Elspeth does."

"Families lie. Get used to it." Olive pushed Xandie out of the chair. "Got people waiting, no lazing around."

Xandie happily paid Olive for the haircut. Who knew the naked wiccans were so creative with hair follicles?

"We have a deal and a truce. As long as you come in for regular hair checks every six weeks."

Holly spoke up before Xandie. "You got it. It's a deal." She shook the hairdressers' hands and skipped out the shop.

Snickering and waving to Dorothy and Olive,

Xandie followed her cousin. She ran straight into the back of the demon-ridden Professor Amoru.

"We must stop meeting like this, Alexandra."

Xandie scooted back, an automatic apology tripping off her tongue. She scrutinized the man in front of her. Snappily dressed in a well-cut dove gray suit, with a stylish midnight blue bow tie. All teamed with a pale cream dress shirt. His silver hair was combed back, and powder blue eyes twinkled with a definite red ring around the pupil. "Are you cataloguing me for any reason, dear child?"

Breaking their stare, she flashed him a blinding smile. "Is there a reason I should scrutinize you?"

The charming Professor's smile didn't waver at all, but his eyes narrowed a tad. "None. Whatever happens I will never harm you or your line. Not now."

Not now? What about before today? Xandie changed the subject. "I had to vacate my house yesterday. Infestation of Imps."

Professor Amoru tisked. "Imps are pernicious creatures when left to annoy their victims."

"Especially when directed by someone."

The professor laughed out loud. "Imps are better when they are given explicit instructions to cause chaos but not injure. Or so I've heard."

"They injured my bra by parachuting and my cat, Theo, was emotionally wounded when they tied him up for target practice with my kitchen knives before I managed to rescue him." Xandie glowered at the demon in men's clothing.

His humor dropped, absent from face and voice. "I'm sure whoever controlled the imps isn't happy to hear the news. But Imps abhor felines, possibly why they may have gone outside their initial orders."

"The imps hated Theo. They were about to use a carving knife."

"I'm sure the master of the imps will correct that oversight. But I very much doubt whether the imps will attack again."

"Because the master didn't get access to the library?" Or because he did?

"Rest assured, librarian. There will be no more incursions of imps for nefarious purposes. I'm sure the master has learned his lesson." Amoru bowed to Xandie and sauntered down the pavement.

Holly popped up behind Xandie. "He wanted to let you know you won't get hurt without admitting it."

"What makes you think 'I won't harm you or your line' comment is honest?"

Holly considered Xandie's words, her eyes unfocused and tinged with silver before turning back to Harrow amber. "Yep, I think he's telling the truth. At least for now. He vibed on Sera. I think their arguing kept him more human. He isn't happy she's gone and who wants an annoyed demon? But that doesn't mean he won't give up any access to the library, he just won't harm you to do it."

"Wise words, cousin of mine, wise words." Xandie linked arms with Holly as they strolled in the opposite direction to Point Muse's resident demon.

For now, she had to focus on the Knight and a way to expose him...

Without it costing her life.

TWELVE

"Elspeth was a bust, but you all got make-overs? Great." Pouting, Lila threw herself down onto a small sofa in Xandie's library.

"Don't you try that with us. The old girls spilled you visit them every six weeks, traitor." Holly pointed an accusing finger at her cousin.

"Good hair, just don't share." Lila fluffed her curly brown locks and posed. "Find a good hairdresser and keep them, even if they're crazy, naked wiccans in a war with your family."

Holly and Xandie looked at each other and shrugged.

Xandie couldn't argue with logic. "You learn anything from Elspeth?" She stroked a purring Theo who'd crawled into her lap.

"Nope. Same stuff as before. But she said he'd had a regard for Sera and would never harm her. Whatever that means."

Holly paced one side of the library. "Means fighting with Sera made him happy. But he's a demon, maybe the same one who burned down the library. Do we trust him?"

Trusting a demon, in Xandie's opinion, sounded like an exercise in futility. But he seemed genuine when he swore he'd never harm Sera or her family. "So, we have the mayor and the Professor, both suspects. Both want access to the library; the question is do they want it bad enough to kill?"

"That's an easy answer to find." Theo jumped down from Xandie's lap and sauntered over the Lila. One mighty bound and he joined her on the couch. He rolled over and presented his tummy for a rub. "If asked the right way, the library can pin down every supernatural creature, their clan, history, weakness etc. in the world. The mayor could use the information to hunt down and exterminate every non-human bloodline. In the demon's case, he could extract information on other demons in the demonic hierarchy and use it to take control."

"He'd control the Underworld or Hell or whatever it's called?" Xandie stared off into space. Both of her suspects had valid motives, but she was missing something. A link, a compelling reason to murder a person in cold blood. Or did she just want her great-aunt's murder to mean something?

This time Lila answered Xandie. "Nope. Not the Underworld. Hades controls that. Demons have a hierarchy. Imps are on the bottom, then second tier demons and then first tier. Next is Admin, commanders, lords and ladies. The top three layers are Grand Dukes, Princes and the emperor. A generalization, but about right." Lila wrinkled her nose. "My dad works for Hades in the Underworld. He sometimes comes into contact with them."

"And Amoru?" Xandie couldn't stand sitting anymore and wandered the shelves, trailing her fingers over book spines and bound scrolls.

Holly slipped into Xandie's space, reclined and closed her eyes. "No clue. But the demon who burned the library had to be a Grand Duke at least."

Thinking the problem through, Xandie picked up a scroll and tapped her chin with it. "They both want access to the library to find supernatural creatures to kill or blackmail. But how does the library help them do that?" Xandie's necklace warmed against her neck and the scroll she held lifted a little in her hands.

Taking the hint, she unrolled it. Names, species and whereabouts flickered on the papyrus. Changing position as the subject listed moved around. This is what the mayor wanted. "An all you can kill supernatural buffet," Xandie muttered.

"Excuse you?" Lila frowned at the strange comment.

She showed them the scroll. "I must have picked up the library's vibes, and without thinking, grabbed this scroll. It lists supernatural creatures and their whereabouts in real time. And it includes demons and who they inhabit while they visit the earth plane."

"Gold for human or demon." Holly opened her eyes. "Does this mean Amoru and the mayor are level pegging as suspects? What about the Professor's non-aggression oath to you and your line?"

Lila weighed in. "Doesn't have to hurt her to get the scroll or access to the library. He just needs to get Xandie out of the way for a while and convince the library to let him in. What's the plan?"

"A trap." Xandie hid the scroll behind a copy of the *'Carnivorous Eating Habits of Unicorns.'* "We need to entice both of the suspects out with bait. Have Braun and his shifter minions standing by to deal with them afterward."

Holly stared worriedly at her cousin. "Bait?"

"Me and the scroll. I'll tell them I know who they are and offer them the scroll for the best price."

"No way." Lila shook her head. "They won't believe you'd cave for money."

"Not money, protection. And my job. I'll tell them I want safety from Sanguis reprisals. My condition will be the safety of Point Muse residents and my family. It'll make it more believable."

"Might work," Lila mused. "But we have to get the messages to our suspects and sort out protection in case everything goes sideways. But Braun will stop you if he gets wind of the plan too soon."

"That's why we set up the meet with the suspects and then tell Braun just before show time. He gets to our meet in enough time to back us up but not stop it." Xandie held up her phone. "We have to hope our phones are working and decided when and where to meet. Any ideas?"

Lila raised a hand like a kid in school. "What about the old drive-in outside town? It's abandoned and the kids use it for hooking up, but no one should be there during the week. Plenty of room for the shifters to take the suspects down. Also, it's outside of town if the demon gets frisky."

Agreeing, Holly sat up and flicked through her

phone. "Elspeth put a boost spell on my phone, so the ley lines don't affect the reception too much. She should be able to design a potion or a ritual which binds a human or a demon in case of any issues."

"Remind me to get that boost from Elspeth. The lack of reception in Point Muse drives me crazy. Right, we have a where sorted. What about when?" Satisfaction seeped into Xandie's bones. This was a plan. The right course of action provided the knight and the demon didn't kill her.

"What about tomorrow? Let's say Thursday at the drive-in at one a.m. No entrance fee needed." Holly snickered.

"Why one in the morning, Cuz?" Lila wandered over to Holly and whacked her on the back of her head. "That's for a poor attempt at a joke. We expect better from a mouthy Harrow."

"Ow." Holly rubbed the spot on the back of her head and glowered at Lila. "Midnight is too clichéd, eleven p.m. is too early, one it is."

"It's a date." Xandie smirked at her banshee cousin. "Since you find the situation hilarious, you get to call Braun and give him the details just before we go." Xandie sure as heck wasn't volunteering to call the bane of her life, Police Chief Braun. "I'll do the mayor. Lila can contact the Professor and Elspeth for the binding spell." Not waiting for her cousins, she dialed the mayor's number. The library should boost the signal enough for the call to go through. Wouldn't be much of a trap if no one turned up.

"The mayor's office. Irene Cummings here," frosty tones iced the line.

"Xandie Meyers from the library. I'd like to pass on an urgent message to the mayor."

"And?"

The spinster wasn't giving an inch. "I know who the mayor is. *Equis. Pura. Sanguis.*" Xandie recited the Knights Sanguis Latin motto. "I want to barter my safety and that of the Point Muse residents for a scroll stating the movements of all supernatural creatures." *Take the bait, Irene.*

"Go on."

Hooked. "Meeting is Thursday, one a.m., at the old drive-in. I'll bring the scroll, but the mayor has to come alone." Xandie hung up the phone and wiped her palms on her jeans. She turned to her cousins and mimed a victory dance.

"I hope you know what you're doing," Theo hissed at Xandie.

"It's my plan. If everyone follows it, nothing will

go wrong." Xandie smiled, impressed by her plan-making skills.

"Famous last words. And I mean last." Theo marched off, his tail swinging.

"We're all going to die," Lila moaned as the three girls crouched behind the abandoned snack bar counter at the drive-in.

"Holly hasn't screamed yet." Xandie peered close at Holly's eyes. Not a speck of silver covered the pupils. "Nope, all good."

Holly blinked while she shoveled popcorn into her mouth.

"Although she may be in a butter popcorn coma." Xandie poked at chipmunk Holly's puffed-out cheeks.

Arching an eyebrow, Holly swallowed a mouthful of buttery goodness. "Can't help it. It's this or donuts and I want to do my jeans up tomorrow."

Lila liberated a handful of popcorn from Holly. "How about you don't bring any food at all?"

"How about you get your face out of my popcorn," Holly hissed back, teeth bared at her cousin.

Rubbing her forehead, Xandie pulled the carton of popcorn out of Holly's hand and dumped it on the ground behind her. "There, now the only eating will be the imps if they turn up. They can overdose their arteries on butter and choke to death. Now can we focus on our murder suspects?"

Holly and Lila sniffed together and then ignored each other.

"Holly, did you get hold of Braun and let him know the plan?" Xandie nibbled her lip. If she was honest, she was a tad nervous about tonight. Having Braun as back up, as much as it pained her to admit, made her more positive about tonight's outcome.

"He was out policing. But Aggie said she'd pass the message on. She also said they'd be there even if they had to swim through a lake of honey." She considered Aggie's words for a moment. "I have no clue what that means, but she sounded serious."

"No Braun for the moment. We need to stall."

"That may be a problem." Lila pointed to the figure walking toward the meeting spot. "Someone turned up early."

The three girls dropped below the counter in the old snack bar.

Xandie raised her head and squinted. The demon needed to walk straight into the binding circle they'd etched with the blessed chalk Elspeth had dug up for them. The trap would hold the demon until they gave the sign to Elspeth who'd deliver him back to his demonic buddies...supposedly? Not that Xandie had ever dealt with a demon before. But Theo was confident it would work. A cat confident blessed chalk would hold a demon. *Yep. Not a normal day.*

"It's Amoru. I can feel him tonight." Holly's eyes shivered silver.

Xandie shuddered. *That phrase wasn't creepy at all.* Taking a deep breath, she stood. Lila shoved the fake scroll provided by the library into her hands. Xandie stepped away from the old snack shack and shuffled toward the demon trap. Taking her time, she pulled up at the edge of the trap. The chalk they'd used was barely visible in the muted glow of the lights they'd rigged up. Professor Amoru had dressed in a dinner suit with a snazzy blue bow tie.

He bowed his silver-lined head in a formal welcome. "Greetings, Alexandra. Are you sure you should take this course of action?" He arched an eyebrow. "Sera would not have approved. Theo must be leading you astray."

Theo had already coughed multiple fur balls into her shoes to show his displeasure. He was afraid she'd compromise the library, and he'd lose another librarian. "You don't want the scroll?" Xandie lifted it above her head in query.

He tracked the movement. "If you give, I will receive. This mission has consumed my being for a long time." His eyes gleamed red, before settling back to plain blue.

"So, you're a demon? Did you kill the man you're inside of? Did you kill my great-aunt?" Xandie lowered her arm; her grand gesture seemed a little stupid now.

"Ah, my child." Amoru sighed and shuffled closer to the chalk circle. "I have had many bodies, some willing and others not. But this one was a gift or a curse from the library herself. I can remain on earth in this form without shifting. But I must live as a human to use it. The library permits small magics, like the imps." He chuckled for a moment. "I did not expect the antics of underwear-parachuting denizens of Hell. But big magic will force me back to the demonic life of body hopping."

"Why did Sera do that for you?" Maybe her great-aunt had liked the demon more than she'd let on to those around her.

"Sera didn't, the library did. It has forgiven me for burning her down, I think."

"And my great-aunt? Did you kill her to get access to the library?"

He flung his hands in the air in human frustration. "Do you think the library would permit me a body if I had killed her librarian? Sera and I crossed swords, but the fighting made both of our lives less boring. I never hurt her." He held his hands, palms up, out to Xandie. "Access is paramount, but I do not want to hurt you and I never touched a hair on Sera's head."

Xandie believed his words and her necklace tightened around her throat. The library must agree with his words as well. But they still had to follow the plan. If it wasn't the demon, it had to be the mayor. Xandie waved the scroll. "Fine, I believe you. Here's the scroll. Come and take it."

With a curious smile on his face, equal parts pride and mischief, he stepped into the circle and stopped. "A binding circle with blessed chalk?" He dropped his head back and guffawed deep bellows of delight. "Elspeth. So entertaining."

"This circle means you can't shift or leave. If you didn't kill Sera that means our other suspect did. But I need you here in the circle, so I don't get distracted. I promise we'll let you out," Xandie pleaded with

Amoru. The last things she needed were a grumpy demon stalking her.

"This is a dangerous game you play, child. Make sure it doesn't come back and stab you. But I can't fault your need for justice for Sera." He smiled his acceptance.

Xandie nodded to Amoru and stepped back from the circle, careful not to smudge the chalk lines.

She headed toward the other side of the lot where they had another circle etched. This time one to bind and hold a human. As Xandie skirted the snack shack, she spared a glance for where her cousins had hidden behind the counter. No sign. Hopefully this meant Lila and Holly had snuck off to find Braun and tell him they had a demon trapped. She'd have to delay the mayor until the bear cavalry arrived.

There was no hint. No sound of footsteps. The sound of metal grinding on metal and the sting of a sharp blade slicing her skin was her first sign the knight had ambushed her.

"I must say, you have wrapped this whole situation up for me."

A woman's cold tones froze Xandie's blood. "But the mayor?" It had to be him.

"Please, my brother would never have the guts to do what was necessary."

"You mean kill people."

Irene giggled. Her sword tip wobbled a fraction and Xandie held her breath. Irene's whole demeanor changed. In black clothing, with a sword and a backbone, she was a fearsome enemy.

"Eradicate impure bloodlines. The earth is for humans, not the corrupted. Those are the lessons my father taught me." Irene tore the scroll from Xandie's hand. "And this scroll will help me achieve my mission *and* secure my knighthood within the Sanguis."

Xandie had never noticed before, but the plain gold ring Irene wore had the same inscription of the Sanguis motto. "I thought your brother was the knight."

Irene lowered the sword with one hand and gripped the scroll tight with the other. "Everyone always does. But my father trained me as his successor, not him. Nigel was my cover until the council of Sanguis ratified my name. But they demanded I prove myself and this scroll will do that." Irene unrolled the scroll, hissing when the forgery was revealed. "You think you can play me like the demon? *Think again.* In fact, with you as bait I'm sure the library will give me access." She threw the scroll away and raised her sword, bringing the hilt down on Xandie's head.

Black spread from the outside of Xandie's vision inward, until the last she saw was Irene, Knight Sanguis, smirking with her shark teeth on show. The woman had no clue about good sportsmanship.

If you win, don't rub it in.

THIRTEEN

With clarity came pain. Xandie opened one eye and groaned, a heavy metal band digging into her head. She rolled over onto her side and gagged. Flattening her hands on the wooden floor, she attempted to push herself upright.

Hang on... Wood?

The last thing she remembered was the old drive-in. Trying to focus, Xandie peered around. The antique white walls of the library anteroom met her gaze. She'd woken up right where Irene Cummings had staked her lawyer.

"It's poetic. A stake through his eye. He was descended from seers, you know." Irene waggled her fingers in a creepy villainous hello, her sword now belted to her side.

Coughing, Xandie scooted back until she sat against a wall. "And Louise Maker, my real estate agent?"

"Oh, that one. Single-minded woman. She was an elemental witch. Lightning was her special gift."

"So, you electrocuted her?" She scanned the room for Theo, but he was noticeably absent. The inside door to the library remained closed, but as she watched, it inched open a tad and her necklace warmed. The library wanted her to go inside. But why? Irene would be on Xandie in a flash.

"Appropriate, I thought. The banker took some planning. He's descended from King Midas, so he had to die in a gold-related incident. Difficult, but in the end—*his end*—a golden cranberry and ginseng muffin laced with water hemlock from the library's own garden had to do. I wasn't pleased with that, but one sometimes has to make do."

Yep, loony tune. Xandie kept an eye on the door as it opened further. This time she glimpsed Theo's tail and an imp smirking and waving at her. The library must have a plan. She just had to keep the villain monologuing and find out what it was. "And my great-aunt Sera?"

Irene slapped her hand on her leg. "That woman. Such an annoyance. She never let me near the library. And Amoru dropped me like I was poison when he met her. I decided that would be a perfect way for Sera to go...*poison*." Irene grimaced. "I'd miscalculated though, I didn't realize Sera had appointed an heir already. My brother failed to tell me in time. But I got there."

"Yeah, and only four people had to die. No harm, no foul...*not*."

"Well, it's a tad more than four people killed. I've purified the Point Muse area off and on since we moved here over twenty years ago. My brother, Nigel, is support and cleanup crew, since he hasn't got the stomach for the kill. In fact..." She paused for effect. "I almost had you when you were five. Would have solved this whole mess. But your mother and her Harrow instincts saved you."

Xandie had been right about her mother's disappearance and about the identity of the killer knight. She just had the wrong Cummings.

"Is my mom alive?" Xandie knew it was pointless. Knew her mother was dead after all this time, but one little kernel of hope remained.

Irene tittered, holding a hand with manicured nails over her mouth. "Oh, my, no. I don't expect so. After she told you to run, she darted off in the opposite direction and misjudged the edge of the cliff. I felt cheated, but it made clean up much easier. Even became a mysterious disappearance. One time my brother didn't mess up a mission. Although he lost you. I sometimes wonder if he did it on purpose," Irene mused.

A wave of red-hot heat washed over Xandie. Her mother was really gone. She stamped the pain into the back of her heart. She didn't have time for hurt unless it meant putting it on Irene. An imp stuck its head out of the library door and chittered to Xandie, encouraging her to move. Xandie pushed against the wall and rose, weaving, to face her mother's killer. "You're psychotic. Didn't your parents ever discipline you?"

The strong killer attitude dropped, and Irene screamed at Xandie, "My mother was useless, my father got rid of her taint early. Saw her weakness and my brother was just like her. I had no choice, one of us had to stand and fight. My father was hard, but he knew he had to prepare me for the coming war. The war to eradicate all corrupted lines from this world. It will be a biblical purging and you won't survive." Irene spat the words at Xandie. Her hands curled into claws as she scrabbled at Xandie's neck, trying to choke her words away.

"Geez, say it, don't spray it." Xandie wiped her

face with one hand. The other she inched toward a chair the library had replaced after her lawyer died. She flung it hard at Irene. Not bothering to wait and see wood against face results, Xandie bolted for the library. Slamming the door behind her, she ran to the back of the library, and crouched, waiting for the library to bring the pain on the psycho wannabe knight. An imp dropped onto her shoulder, and chittered away, pointing at the door. The library would surely lock Irene out or incapacitate her. Instead the library door slammed open and Irene strode in, eyes glittering with a need for blood, her sword arm held high.

"You can't hide from me." She held up Xandie's necklace. "See? I have your connection. I can track you like prey and the library can't help you anymore."

Xandie scrabbled at her neck but her hands met bare skin. She hadn't even felt Irene remove it. The woman was right; the library couldn't help her now.

"I wouldn't be so sure of that, toots." Theo bounded off a shelf, aiming at Irene's head. Two imps with minute swords rode the cat like a mighty steed. Tiny, demonic knights coming to her rescue. Theo landed on Irene's shoulder and dragged his claws down her sword arm. The imps cheered and poked her head and neck with their toothpick swords.

Irene screamed and swatted around her head. She dislodged Theo, who flew into a bank of shelves, thankfully filled mainly with papyrus scrolls and not heavy books. The shelf toppled over. The scrolls tumbled down. Theo lay still in the middle of the mess.

Xandie grabbed a pile of books and pegged them at Irene's head. "Not my damn cat too."

The library agreed with Xandie and the room shuddered for a moment. The walls shivered and shelving rattled wildly. Even with Xandie watching the walls, they still extended. The room elongated until a corridor of shelving and books were between her and her mother's killer.

"I think the library disagrees with you on not helping me," she hollered back at Irene. Using the woman's distraction, Xandie scooted over to Theo to check on the brave feline. She pulled a book off him. An imp hung spread-eagle underneath. He grimaced and waved his sword at her. Easing the tired warrior off Theo, she patted the cat's sweat-soaked fur. "Anyone one would think you like me, Theo, if you keep leaping to my rescue."

Theo groaned and opened one eye. "Fresh tuna

might help me mend. I'm sure I've broken every bone in my tail."

"I might be able to work that out." Xandie grinned, relieved. Theo would be fine if he resorted to emotional blackmail.

"Well, I've worked it out. You're about to die." Irene panted above Xandie. Her raised sword glinted, a silent testament to the hate beaming from her crazed eyes.

The lights in the library flickered as hundreds of tiny imps swarmed out of the light fittings. All hoisted tiny toothpick swords above their heads. Xandie swore she heard a *Geronimo* and a *tally ho* in amongst their chittering. They swarmed up Irene's legs. She screamed a high-pitched wail and flung her sword around. Xandie ducked and scooted out of sword reach, Theo and the wounded imp in her arms.

Dragon's breath flamed through the library, avoiding the books and scrolls. And vines twinned their way around and through every library nook and cranny. The roar of a bear vibrated through the cavernous room. A group of figures advanced down the long library-made corridor. Xandie smiled. Her friends were coming to the rescue. Her family was here to defend her; even the interfering dragons had turned up for a fight. Xandie looked around the room. Her library defended her with the help of a plague of battle-hardened imps. Looks like Amoru escaped their circle after all if his imps were battling Irene.

Speaking of Irene...

Clambering to her feet with Theo and the imp cuddled into her chest, Xandie stepped up to the imp-covered mound known as Irene. The only spare flesh the imps weren't covering was her face. The imp-bound woman radiated crazy even covered in the denizens of Hell.

"I should have hunted you down when I had the chance. Shouldn't have allowed my brother to talk me into letting you go. I will get out and slaughter you and every impure I can find. Equis. Pura. Sanguis." She yelled the last word but gurgled to a stop when an imp sat on her face and passed wind. Giggling, a mob of imps presented their backsides and tooted a lullaby to calm the crazy woman.

"Looks like you have the matter in hand."

Braun's rough tones washed over Xandie and for once she didn't feel like battering him over the head with a hard object. He must have shifted to bear before charging in to rescue her. He still had huge hunched shoulders and massive non-human sized arms. Braun obviously still had his bear sense of smell as he leaned over and snuffled her honey shampoo-washed hair.

"The imps have it in hand, or horns, for that matter. I take it from their presence our demon professor escaped our binding circle?"

"Elspeth let him out." Amelia frowned at Chief Braun as Xandie's aunt drew level with the duo. "You have a little fur there." She pointed to his mono brow.

Zach Braun blushed and nodded to Xandie. "Glad you're okay." He smiled for a moment. "At least this time it was self-defense." He waved at her and joined the rest of his family as they lumbered out.

Amelia and Winifred each gave Xandie a hug. She watched while Lila and Holly and a host of her Harrow relatives dealt with the vines and flowers. The library shuddered and everyone held their breath when it shivered back into a normal large room. "What happens to the pyscho with a sword?"

Elspeth pried Amelia and Winifred away from Xandie. "Give the girl breathing space. She's survived one murder attempt; she doesn't need another." Elspeth cackled and took a step back to get a good look at the battered Xandie. "Braun wanted to take Cummings in, but I called a favor in with a guy I know. He's a Templar, and they're excited to get their knightly hands on a Cummings. Her bloodline has murdered impures for a long time." Elspeth pointed toward Lila and Holly. Behind them, a bearded figure in a long trench coat hovered. He looked normal, but when he moved Xandie glimpsed silver armor under the coat. "He came prepared to deal with her, but you and the imps had already completed his mission."

Xandie demurred. "All the library, Theo and the imps doing."

"Well, dearie, whoever helped you, you're safe. We heard Irene talk about your mother. You found justice for her and saved the library and the residents of Point Muse. Not a bad week's work."

Had it only been a week? Xandie followed her family out of the library and into the kitchen to brew a calming Harrow tea. She'd found a family, friends, a talking cat and now a pet imp.

It had only taken a few murders to find her place.

FOURTEEN

Xandie kicked back and polished off another butter puff before taking a large sip of her hot chocolate. Lila's bakery was back to bustling. Customers stacked in for her cousin's latest creation involving cream, pastry, honey and spun sugar. All the Braun family were lined up with money already out. Xandie shook her head. *Bears and honey.* She snorted to herself and demolished another puff. Winifred and Holly pushed their way in and collapsed in chairs around Xandie's table.

Holly laid her head on the table and pretended to snore.

"New job tiring you out?" Her cousin had started a new job at the Elysian Fields Funeral Home the day after Xandie's epic showdown with

Irene, AKA psycho wannabe with her own sword. Three days later it looked like Holly hadn't had a wink of sleep.

"They put me on flowers. I hate flowers and they hate me. If I see any more of those black roses or white lilies, I might hurl." Holly pouted, pretending to look like a sulky little girl.

Winifred slapped Holly on the back. "Cheer up, no one's tried to kill you girls yet. That's a good start to the new week."

"But they elected Elspeth the new mayor. What good can come from giving extra power to a senile Harrow?" Holly glared at her mother. "I can't believe you voted for her. She calls your only daughter death girl."

"It's a term of endearment." Winifred soothed Holly and gave a wave to her sister, Amelia, behind Lila's counter.

Grandma Elspeth, the new mayor, was an interesting choice for Point Muse. She didn't give it too long before a mob of residents holding flaming torches forced Elspeth from the position. But since the mayor had done a runner and was in the wind, hiding from the police, shifters and Templars, maybe a temporary replacement wasn't such a bad idea.

Xandie leaned back in her chair and stretched

her food belly out. Sera's and her mother's murders avenged, the library, Theo and his new pet imp settled back in and a private oath from the demon Amoru not to harm her was in place. Everything was falling back into normal life. She'd found her niche in the world as a crazy librarian to a sentient library in a town of supernatural creatures. Who'd have thought?

The only loose end was her father. But she'd deal with him when she had the energy. The last thing she wanted was to lose another parent even if it was only to hurt feelings. And everything seemed quiet. The town was peaceful and not a dead body in sight.

Holly's eyes iced over, silver forming an opaque fog over her eyes. The same process every time she saw an impending death...

Here we go again.

The End.

Want More?

You can sign up for my mailing list. It's for new releases and no spam. Be the first to grab specials, new releases and freebies.

Sign up now.

https://www.kellyethan.com/newsletter

THE DASTARDLY DRAGON SLAYER
AND THE POISONED BREATH:
BOOK TWO

There's a murder in the art gallery, a dragon slayer on the loose and a nosy librarian turned sleuth.

Let the mayhem begin...

Xandie Meyers thought she'd found her place in the supernatural world when she moved to Point Muse, Maine. She even made new friends in the form of one Priss Makepeace. But instead of settling into a peaceful new life, Xandie's dealing with rampaging zombie gnomes, bad luck, and now a poisoned dragon body has turned up in the art gallery.

The Dragon clan is snarling for vengeance and her new friend is the prime suspect.

Xandie has no choice but to let Sherlock librarian swing into action before an innocent woman is jailed for a crime she didn't commit and Point Muse dissolves into chaos.

Can Xandie survive long enough to navigate her freaky new world? Or will things that go bump in the night have her for a midnight snack?

If you like snarky dialogue, murder, and mayhem then you'll love the next instalment in Kelly Ethan's Point Muse Mysteries, a new cozy paranormal mystery series.

Unlock the mayhem of The Dastardly Dragon Slayer and the Poisoned Breath!

LEAVE A REVIEW

Did you like this book?
Please leave a review for it on Amazon!

The Killer Knight and the Murderous Chairleg

https://www.amazon.com/gp/product/B083JRTP34/

ABOUT THE AUTHOR

I want to thank everyone who spent the time to read my novel.

My world is small town magic, mystery and mayhem, with plenty of snarky laughs along the way.

With an overactive imagination and a love of all things that go bump in the night, it was natural to write cozy paranormal mysteries, but I also love paranormal romance. No matter the genre, I love sarcastic heroines who like to save the day and solve the puzzle.

With a busy and chaotic household, writing is my outlet for madness. I live in Australia and when not writing, I can be found plotting my next fictional murder or chasing after the family's ferocious hellhound.

Visit me today at my website or say hello on
Facebook or Twitter.

Website:
https://www.kellyethan.com

ALSO BY KELLY ETHAN

COZY PARANORMAL MYSTERY:

Point Muse Cozy Paranormal Mystery Series

The Wicked Witch and the Christmas Chaos

#0 The Pernicious Pixie and the Choked Word

#1 The Killer Knight and the Murderous Chairleg

#2 The Dastardly Dragon Killer and the Poisoned Breath

#3 The Murderous Monster and the Stony Gaze

#4 The Cursed Crow and the Deadly Hex

#5 The Slanderous Siren and the Grievous Gift

#6 The Vengeful Villain and the Cursed Treasure

Lila Harrow: A Point Muse Cozy Paranormal Mystery

#1 Cupcakes, Corpses and Chaos

#2 Pies, Potions and Peril

PARANORMAL ROMANCE:

Miss Predictable.

Mr Muse.

Mr and Mrs Monster

NON FICTION

Heart and Craft.